MINE! MINE!

Favorite Things in My Room
- My bed (It's kind of sunken in the middle, but it's cozy.)
- My desk (It's kind of messy.)
- My computer (Charley gave it to me this summer.)
- My collection of weird gifts from weird relatives I have never met
- My XO Dollz, made by Ninny

DO NOT

Things I Have Never Done
- Sent a text message
- Gone swimming
- Eaten in a restaurant
- Learned to ride a bike
- Been farther away from my house than the local MegaMart

IF YOU'RE READING THIS, STOP NOW!!

Places I Have Never Been
(This list could fill pages, but I will limit it to a few.)
- A foreign country
- The ocean
- A museum
- The mall
- A city

STOP HERE!

Favorite Places
- My room
- MegaMart
- My hiding spot in the school library (I don't get out much.)

Favorite Pastimes
- Snacking
- Watching movies
- Reading
- Writing
- Rearranging my room
- Daydreaming
- Cooking with Ninny

PRIVATE!!!

KEEP OUT!!

Greatest Fears
- Bats
- Deep water
- Speaking out loud
- Public embarrassment
- That I will never be able to leave this town

GO AWAY!!

BEWARE DO NOT TURN THIS PAGE! YOU'LL BE SORRY.

MINE!!

Dear Abigail,
Happy Tridecennary!
Here's a new journal for
you to continue recording
the early life of the
future world-famous Abigail
Thaddeus. (And you'd
better remember me
when you're famous.)
Your friend always,
Charley

Thanks, Charley!
World famous?
I guess I can have
dreams, right?
Ha-ha!

Dear Reader,
In our wonderfully old and creaky house, hidden behind a
small door, we found many volumes of Abigail Thaddeus's
journal. This is the first. We have no idea where she is now,
nor do any of the residents of our town. The whereabouts
of Abigail are as unknown as the many fantastical beasts
she wrote about in this very book. Her life is quite a
mystery, and we hope to solve it. Maybe you can help us.
Sincerely,

Stephanie Brockway & Ralph Masiello

The Mystic Phyles

BEASTS

To the Readers at Ayer Public Library!

Embrace the Doom! Dave!

Ralph Masiello 2011

Mine! Mine! All mine!

THIS JOURNAL BELONGS TO:

Abigail Thaddeus ... is on Facebook!

‹›‹ Charlesbridge

Every good mystery starts off with a map of the town where the mysterious events take place.

MY LIFE (PART 1)

My birthday: October 13. (Today!) It also happens to be "National Face Your Fears Day." I sometimes wonder if this isn't partly to blame for my lot in life. Had I been born a day earlier on "National Kick Butt Day," I might be a totally different person. *Sigh.*

My age: 13. As of today I'm an official teenager. The only benefit so far is that Pop is allowing me to walk to school unsupervised—one less thing for Kane Thornley to torment me about.

Where I live: In an itty-bitty town called Westbrook, in a broken-down old mansion that could also qualify as a minimum-security prison. I figure this might give me points toward fame. The best stories always have a heroine trapped in a creepy old mansion, right?

My family: My grandfather, Pop (the prison guard), and Ninny, my weird-but-lovable grandmother. My mom died when I was born, and my dad died in a fire in this house when I was two. Kind of bad luck for a kid. So I live with my grandparents. Oh, and Peanut. How can I forget my faithful dog, Peanut? He's a gargantuan cloud of black fur who needs to follow me everywhere I go in this house, even the bathroom. *(Spits dog fur out of mouth.)*

This officially begins my first teenage journal. Thanks, Charley! Who knew that I'd actually have something to write about other than what I ate, read, and watched on TV?

HERE IS THE NOTE!

Find the great beasts
under lock and key,
asleep for many an age.
Among stacks on shelves,
they await your eyes
to release them
from the page.

Someday I may look back on this as the note that forever changed my life. (Cue dramatic music here.)

Thursday, oct. 13 {7:00pm}

Today was the weirdest birthday ever. No, weird doesn't even BEGIN to describe it. It started normally: Peanut slobbered all over my cereal, Ninny thought it was the Fourth of July and insisted I wear something patriotic, and I survived school. Then came the weirdness.

Weird Thing No. 1: A black cat followed me after school. About a block from home, it sat down in front of me and stared. Something was hanging from its collar, so I bent down to get a better look. It was a small envelope with my initials on it! My first thought: stupid joke from the creep, Kane Thornley. It would be so like him to send me another gross dead thing. Last week he put a note in my locker with an old dried-up worm inside. The note said: "Princess of Darkness, you've wormed your way into my heart." Ugh.

Black cat of doom.

Inside the envelope was a poem and a little key. It was pretty easy to decipher the poem. "Great beasts" and "release them from the page" had to mean a book about beasts. "Under lock and key ... among stacks on shelves" would have to mean it was either locked up at the library or at Bilbo's Books, the used bookstore. But "stacks on shelves" sounded very library-like. I wished Charley wasn't at home sick. Part of me was totally excited, and part of me—my left armpit—broke out into a sweat. But since my major complaint in life is that nothing ever happens to me, I took a deep breath, decided to risk getting home late, and ran to the library.

Weird Thing No. 2: When I found Miss Malkin, the librarian, I managed to blurt out something about old books and a research paper. (Whenever I need to speak to anyone other than Charley or Ninny, something short-circuits and both my mouth and brain seize up and go faulty. It can be quite problematic at times.) Miss Malkin pursed her wrinkly lips, raised an eyebrow at me, and led me downstairs to Special Collections.

There must have been a billion books in that room. I didn't have much time, but I had the little key. At the back of the room, there were a bunch of dusty cabinets, so I tried the key in each one. Of course, it fit into the very LAST one. (It's always that way in the movies, isn't it?) There, all alone in its crusty glory, was a big old book. The cover read "Bestiary Masielus."

Weird Thing No. 3: Inside the book was a letter for ME!!!!!!!! I didn't have time to read it because by then my right armpit was sweating, too, and I didn't want to get yelled at for being late. So I put the bestiary back and ran home just in time to—guess what?—get yelled at for being late. Pop is SO uptight. As usual, I didn't have the courage to argue, and I didn't want to upset Ninny because she was making my special Fourth of July dinner. So I just clenched my teeth, set the table, and helped Ninny decipher her recipes so that dinner would be edible.

Dinner turned out okay. It was ribs and baked beans. My Fourth of July Surprise Cake was questionable, since Ninny forgot what the surprise was. Poor Ninny. I unwrapped some presents. My favorite was the XO Doll Ninny made for me. She makes me one every year. They're a little weird, but I love them. I also got socks, a super-absorbent hair wrap from the TV shopping channel (Ninny is addicted), and a Russian nesting doll from my great aunt Anya. She always sends me something unusual. Normally I love opening presents, but I was DYING to get up to my room to read that letter . . .

Now for The Letter!

Okay, so this letter is THE biggest shocker of my life. Not that I have much to compare it to, which makes it that much more of a shocker. I had pretty much resigned myself to a life of sheltered monotony, living each day with the secret hope that something unexpected would sweep me away into a life of fame and glory, where I would become magnificent—with a mouth and brain that functioned simultaneously.

The only problem with becoming magnificent is that I've never done anything special. Except for shopping at the MegaMart, I've never been anywhere outside of this town. So I have serious doubts about my capacity for any kind of magnificence, especially since I have only one friend and, according to the Britneys, am a boring nothing. By all outward appearances, I guess I am. Does it count if your whole personality exists only inside your brain?

7

Dearest Abigail,

Happy Birthday. Circumstances have forced me into seclusion in a faraway land, so I must remain anonymous.

I need your help, Abigail. I cannot reveal the reason but only stress its importance. This may seem unusual, and no doubt you will wonder what benefit it will provide me. All will be revealed in time.

What I'd like you to do is research. You will start with mythical beasts. This bestiary will help you. Find as much information as you can. Educate yourself. Investigate the mysteries, then discern for yourself the fact and fiction.

I will contact you again soon. Send word of your progress via the cat. It's very important for you to begin this research. But even more important, tell no one!

I realize this is all very strange. If you pay attention, you may start to find that all is not as it seems.

With my sincerest thanks,

Your Devoted Friend

But now, today, I get this letter from a mysterious Devoted Friend, who appears to be in dire need of my help. What a weird way to help someone in a faraway land. Doing research doesn't really sound dangerous though, except for the fact that someone with a trained cat is watching me. Creepy. I asked Peanut what he thought. He just licked my nose. I need to call Charley now.

Later {8:30pm}

Charley sounded like he was going to hack up a lung when he answered the phone. Between coughing fits, the first thing he asked was if I studied for the algebra test. Ugh! I totally forgot about the algebra test. Anyway, I told him to forget about the algebra test because I had BIG news. I read him the letter. He was speechless, which, for Charley, is amazing.

First we wondered if I should show the letter to Pop. Then Charley calculated that there was a 99.9 percent chance Pop would freak out, rip the letter to shreds, and lock me in my room for the rest of my life.

Then we wondered, if this is so important, why ask a kid like me? Why not a grown-up? Or someone like Charley, who's a walking encyclopedia? We're stumped on that one.

And I'm supposed to keep it a secret. If that's not a gigantic red flag, I don't know what is. But this letter is the most exciting thing that's ever happened to me! How can I not do what it says?

But for now, I must study algebra. I need a snack, though—maybe another piece of Surprise Cake.

Red flag of doom.

MY LIFE (PART 2)

NOTE THIS, TOO: Before I venture any further, I probably should finish this whole background-of-my-life-for-posterity thing. I really should be studying for that algebra test.

My school: Westbrook Junior High. There are 44 kids in my grade, who fit into roughly six camps: Jocks, Art Geeks, Band Geeks, Brains, Kane Minions, and the Britneys. I don't really fit anywhere.

My friends: Charlton Winkley III, aka Charley. That's it. My one friend. He lives next door with his grandparents. His parents are international art dealers, so they travel a lot. Poor Charley. He's always sick and never gets to go with them. He's also allergic to everything—I mean *everything*. I've known Charley for as long as I can remember, and he's always been part of the Brain camp. He's supersmart. But this year he began a self-improvement program to change his reputation. For his health, he's taking megavitamins and drinking weird algae drinks. In hopes of becoming a Band Geek (which, surprisingly, is a step up from the Brains), he's learning to play the tuba in the marching band. I don't want to tell him, but despite Charley's heroic efforts to change his fate, I doubt that popularity is within his reach. Once you're classified, that's it.

Why I'm a poor dejected eighth grader with only one friend: In a small school, it's really hard to get past certain stigmas associated with certain incidents that transpired in elementary school, where I was teased mercilessly and forced into social exile.

My Creepy House
and Other
Weird Stuff

Friday, Oct. 14 {4:15pm}

The algebra test was really hard. I stayed up too late working on my journal pages in preparation for fame and glory. *Sigh.* I know, it's silly.

School dance tonight, but lifeless me is NOT going, of course. Did I mention yet that Kane Thornley is the biggest creep on the face of the planet?

Today at lunch, he and his minions descended upon me for some *torture du jour.* (That's French for senseless torment.) In this stupid Dracula voice, he said, "Abigail, vill you dance vit me tonight? I vant to dance vit zee Princess of Darkness!" Then he and his minions danced around me as the whole lunchroom broke out into peals of laughter. My left armpit started leaking, and my circuits malfunctioned, and I ran out. I want to KILL him! Why is it I can think of a hundred brilliant comebacks when I'm alone?

Anyway, I need to figure out how to get research materials without getting in trouble with Pop. Need cookies to help me think.

Later {8:00pm}

Just instant-messaged Charley. Here's the plan. We try the library first because it doesn't cost anything. I'm going to have to start sneaking extra coins from Ninny's lunch-money jar if I want any books from Bilbo's. I'll go over to Charley's in the morning because, other than school, it's the only place Pop will let me go alone. And then we'll beg Charley's grandmother to let us go to the library without telling Pop. She knows how strict he is and always tries to "honor his wishes" while I'm over there. Keeping my fingers crossed.

Oh cookie cookie
How I love to say the word,
But love more to eat.

HAIKU

Saturday, oct. 15 {1:30 pm}

Covert Library Operation No. 1 worked! First thing was to ask Miss Malkin to let us back into Special Collections. She's so good with that eyebrow-raising thing. I wanted to show the bestiary to Charley and get copies of the pictures. He wore his surgical mask and antibacterial gloves—to prevent exposure to ancient germs—as he performed his inspection. He informed me that most bestiaries were written in the Middle Ages, but the paintings in this one were too sophisticated for that time period. It's most likely a replica from the 1800s. How does he know these things? All I know is that the pictures are really cool. I copied fifteen in total. I can't understand a word of the text—Charley said it's written in Latin—but some of the beasts I recognize. Some I've never heard of, like the giant spider and the giant bat. (I'm NOT looking forward to researching the bat. I hate bats.)

I looked for books to take out. Found a good one about mermaids, called *Sea Enchantress*, and a couple on sea monsters. I think these will give me a good start.

Later {4:00 pm}

Starting *Sea Enchantress* tonight. I've always imagined mermaids as fish-tailed maidens lounging around, combing their long golden hair, and gazing at their reflections while they sing enchanting songs—kind of like the Britneys. Ugh! I really, really, really want mermaids to have more depth than that.

13

Sunday, Oct. 16 {9:00am}

Over the summer Charley built this computer for me out of spare parts he had lying around. Thank you, Charley! It's going to be very useful. Today I'm going to search online for mermaid references.

Later {2:00pm}

Something really weird just happened. Ninny came into my room and whispered that she had a secret to tell me, but she couldn't remember it. She had a key in her hand and motioned for me to follow her. She unlocked one of the spare rooms and whispered that maybe something in there would help remind her. Pop has never let me in any of the spare rooms because there was too much damage from the fire, and he said I might get hurt. But I didn't see any fire damage in the room, just old furniture, boxes, and books.

Then Pop yelled up the stairs that it was time for Ninny's medicine. She whispered, "Shhh! Keep this key! Don't tell your father!" *My father?* "He hates secrets! Don't tell your grandfather either!" She kissed me on the cheek and shuffled downstairs in her fuzzy slippers. She must have been delirious again.

I emailed Charley to tell him everything.

Even Later {8:00pm}

After dinner Pop disappeared into the basement to work on his old radios or whatever it is he spends hours on every day. I've never been allowed down there. He keeps it locked because there's dangerous stuff—tubes and amps—all over the place. So it was my chance to go back into The Room (that's what I'm affectionately calling the spare room to which I now have a key) for a little while. I can't believe all the boxes. This creepy postcard was in a box of letters.

The Feejee Mermaid

It looks pretty convincing, doesn't it? At first I thought it was totally real, but after a little Internet searching, I found out that back in the 1800s, Japanese fisherman made money by selling these little mermaids to sailors as souvenirs. They sewed monkey bodies to fish tails and then dried them.

Even More Later {8:45pm}

Must forage for snacks. I'm almost out of cookies. We're overdue for a trip to MegaMart. If I don't have snacks, I'll chew on my nails, and I've been trying to break the habit.

I have enough mermaid information to start assembling pages, but I'll have to do that tomorrow. Now it's time for homework. Science lab notes are due. Since Britney #1 is my lab partner this quarter, it's only natural that I'm doing all the work. How is anyone supposed to have a life with all this homework? Oh, silly me. I forgot. I have no life.

My first creature!

Mermaid

> A beast of the sea, wonderfully shapen as a maid from the navel upward and a fish from the navel downward.
> FROM **THE PHYSIOLOGUS**, WRITTEN AROUND 200 CE

A WEE BIT OF MERMAID HISTORY

The very oldest written records of fish-tailed people date back to about 5000 BCE. That's over 7,000 years ago! That's old. But these weren't just any old fish-tailed people. They were gods. Gods! And the first fish-tailed god wasn't a "maid" at all. It was a man. Wow. My first beastly stereotype has been shattered.

This drawing is from a carving, dated around 700 BCE, found on an outer wall of King Sargon II's palace at Khorsabad (in modern-day Iraq). It shows Oannes, Lord of the Waters.

This is one of the copies from the bestiary.

Funny, you don't hear much about mermen these days. I wonder why?

So if the first mermaid was a hairy, hat-wearing fish dude, where did my vision of the cute hair-combing mermaid come from?

If you believe that mermaids are real, the answer is simple: there are both male and female merpeople, end of story.

If you're skeptical, then the history of mermaid myth could be summed up as one really long game of Telephone.

Almost every ancient culture on earth has stories about supernatural beings from the water. Before writing was invented, these stories were passed from person to person. Little by little, fish-tailed gods changed into other types of fish-tailed creatures with strange powers, becoming lovely maidens who sang magical songs. When the sailing ship was invented, people from all over Europe and Asia began to share these stories, especially sailors, who were fond of blaming shipwrecks on mermaids.

WEIRD DREAM

I must have mermaids on the brain. I dreamed that I was sailing with Pop—which is odd because I can't even swim. I was hanging my hair over the side of the boat, watching it swirl around and disappear into the dark water. Then a bluish face floated up through my hair, beckoning me into the water. It was my father. I reached out, then Pop jerked me back into the boat. I tried to scream . . . but I had no mouth. Then I woke up.

Mermaids can foretell the future . . . especially weather. They always seem to appear before storms. No one knows if they cause the storms, or if they try to give warnings.

An Irish mermaid wears a red feathered cap that allows her to breathe underwater. If you steal it, she can't return to the water.

On land, mermaid tails become legs.

Sometimes mermaids save men from shipwrecks. But sometimes they drag them to their deaths at the bottom of the sea!

If you eat a Japanese mermaid (ew!), you will live for 800 years.

If you rescue a mermaid in trouble, she will grant you wishes and riches.

Dang, I dropped a chocolate cupcake here! Ninny and I made cupcakes today to celebrate National Chocolate Cupcake Day.

19

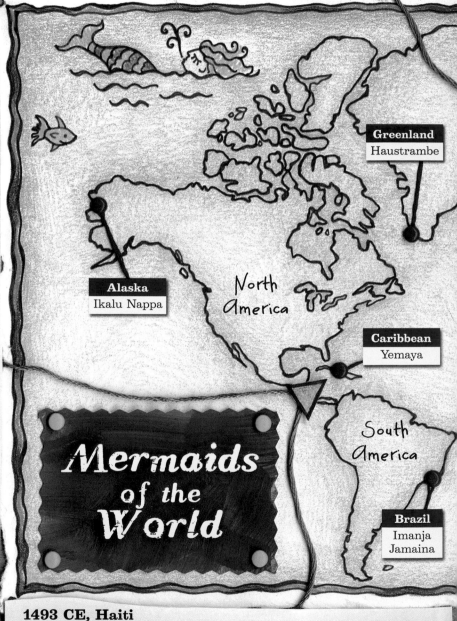

1830 CE, Scotland

A written record described a mermaid's dead body that washed ashore. The creature was "about the size of a well-fed child of three or four years of age . . . the hair was long, dark and glossy, while the skin was white . . . the lower part of the body was like a salmon, but without the scales."

1614 CE, Caribbean Islands

Captain John Smith recorded that he saw a mermaid "swimming about with all possible grace." He said she had "large eyes, rather too round, a finely shaped nose, a little too short . . . and her long green hair imparted to be her original character."

Greenland
Haustrambe

Alaska
Ikalu Nappa

North America

Caribbean
Yemaya

South America

Mermaids of the World

Brazil
Imanja
Jamaina

1493 CE, Haiti

Christopher Columbus recorded that one of his crewmen saw three creatures "who rose very high from the sea, but they are not so beautiful as they are painted."

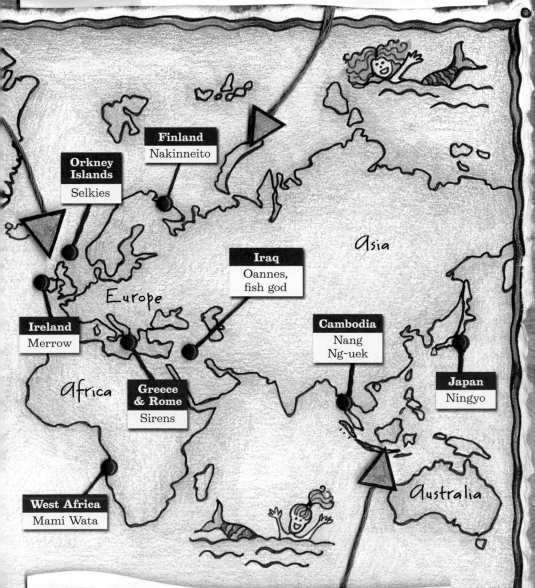

Finland
Nakinneito

Orkney Islands
Selkies

Iraq
Oannes, fish god

Asia

Ireland
Merrow

Europe

Cambodia
Nang Ng-uek

Japan
Ningyo

Africa

Greece & Rome
Sirens

Australia

West Africa
Mami Wata

1717 CE, Borneo
It was recorded that "a monster resembling a siren, caught near the island of Borne . . . it was fifty-nine inches long, and in proportion as an eel. It lived on land, in a vat full of water, during four days seven hours. From time to time it uttered little cries like those of a mouse."

21

My incredibly BRILLIANT {but not very scientific} IDEAS

MERMAIDS COULD IN FACT BE:

1 Sailor's Delusions

Sea life must have been rough. If I was stuck on a smelly ship, with a bunch of smelly sailors, eating smelly food, riding stormy seas day after day, for months on end, I'd be delusional, too!

Hel

2 Sea Mammals

Mermaids could be a case of mistaken identity—confused with dolphins, seals, or dugongs. I have a hard time believing a dugong could look like a lovely maiden. But if you're in a delusional state, due to the conditions described above, I suppose it's possible.

22

Undiscovered Animals

The world is so big, with so many unexplored places, especially in the ocean. Just because a creature hasn't been documented and picked apart by a room of old guys in lab coats doesn't mean it doesn't exist, right?

If mermaids are really discovered someday, I hope they don't look like this.

WHAT IS CRYPTOZOOLOGY?

There's a whole field of study that I'd never heard of. Cryptozoology is the study of unknown animals and the quest to prove they exist. Very cool. Maybe I'll become a cryptozoologist.

Personally, I think if mermaids do exist, their tails are probably more dolphin-like, to keep the whole mammal thing cohesive.

Thursday, oct. 20 {8:30pm}

Whew! Finally finished mermaids in between all my homework this week. I think my pages turned out okay, but I wish I could draw better—more like Deke Stoltz. He's one of the Art Geeks who gets all the ooohs and aaahs from Miss Gretchen, our art teacher.

Let's see, what news do I have to report? Charley is pestering me to try his algae drink. It smells like a lawn, and his skin seems to be turning a slight shade of green. No, thanks.

He got invited to a marching-band party on Saturday. It'll be mostly high school kids, since only a few eighth graders are in the band. He wants me to go. Right. All I'd be able to do is stand around, unable to speak. Even if I wanted to, Pop wouldn't let me out of the house.

Kane's torture continues, and I continue to wish that the floor of the school would open up and swallow him. His new thing this year is "accidentally" bumping into me so hard that I drop all my books. Then while I try to pick them up, he and his minions kick them around the floor. I'm not his only victim though. Last time he did it to Charley, Charley told him that it was really quite sad that he needed to belittle those he perceived as weak in order to make himself feel powerful. Charley got stuffed in a locker. Poor guy.

Just finished my last National Chocolate Cupcake Day cupcake. Need to study for Friday's biology test.

Tiny masterpiece
Of chocolate-frosted cake,
Your beauty is pure.

HAIKU

Friday, oct. 21 {6:00am}

Something weird happened late last night. After I finished studying, I wasn't tired, so I started reading *In the Wake of the Sea Serpents*. By 11:30, I really needed to make a dash for the bathroom. Normally, I hate leaving my room late at night. The house is really creepy in the dark. On the way back to my room, Peanut suddenly went crazy and guess what whooshed over my head? A bat! I screamed, which woke Ninny up, so she screamed too, then ran into the hall and fell over Peanut. Pop must have heard us from the nether regions of the basement, because he came running up the stairs, caught the bat in a towel, and took it up to the attic. I hate bats.

When I asked Ninny why Pop took it up to the attic and didn't just let it go outside, she whispered, "Oh, my dear, it's just not safe for them anymore. Wee Spies are everywhere!" I should've known better than to ask. Ninny's obsessed with spies. She tucked me in, apprehended numerous Wee Spies from under my bed—giant globs of dog fur—then waved her hands around the windows to ward off evil spirits and told Peanut to take good care of me. Good old Ninny. I stayed awake, listening for Pop to come down the stairs. He was up there for over an hour! What the heck was he doing?

Anyway, I woke up this morning with a gigantic zit on my chin. Have nothing to cover it with except an ancient jar of Ninny's makeup. Ugh. At least it's Friday.

Still Friday {10:00 pm}

Eating last bag of potato chips as I read more of *In the Wake of the Sea Serpents*. I hope we go shopping at MegaMart tomorrow. Must get zit cream. Kane tactfully pointed out that an alien was growing on my chin. I hate him.

Checked attic, hoping not to find bats. Door was locked.

Saturday, oct. 22 {12:30 pm}

Went to MegaMart with Ninny and Pop. Bought snacks, cereal, and Super ExZit cream to kill the alien. Ran into Britneys #2 and #3. They did their typical stare-whisper-giggle thing. I wish I could have said something really clever to annoy them. But my mind went blank, as usual, so I just glared. *Sigh.*

Pop descended to his dungeon for the afternoon, so Charley's coming over before he goes to his band party. We're going to explore The Room some more.

Later {3:30 pm}

My mind is boggled by what we found in The Room. First, Charley found a really cool map with all kinds of sea monsters on it. Then I found a box full of Ninny's old travel journals. One entry described a visit she and Pop made to some sultan guy in Turkey, to investigate his gryphon claw. She wrote that the claw was a fraud, but the sultan didn't believe it. He was poisoned two weeks later. Ninny used to tell me this story when I was younger. I always thought it was just some nutty thing she dreamed up, like the Wee Spies being everywhere. But she and Pop actually did visit a sultan!

Sunday, Oct. 23 {10:00am}

Haven't heard from Charley. Wonder how the party went.

A Little Later {10:30am}

Charley emailed. The party was really fun, and he says the band kids are totally cool. I'm happy he had a good time. Really. I am.

Later {7:15pm}

So far I have sea-monster information from two library books and a zillion websites. I found tons on the Internet, but it got really confusing because I didn't keep track of where I found things. When I wanted to go back and look something up, I couldn't remember where it was. From now on, I'll bookmark everything.

The best information came from the book I mentioned earlier: *In the Wake of the Sea Serpents,* by Bernard Heuvelmans. He was a scientist who wanted to prove that sea monsters didn't exist. He researched records of 646 sea-monster sightings around the world, between the years 1639 and 1960, trying to prove that each one was either a regular, known animal or a hoax. He was able to explain most of the sightings. But he didn't expect that there would be a whole bunch that he couldn't explain! More to come. Incidentally, he also invented the word "cryptozoology"!

Even Later {8:30pm}

Ninny asked me if I found anything to jog her memory about the secret. I asked if a postcard with a shriveled-up mermaid, a map of sea monsters, and a journal entry about a gryphon claw rang any bells. She said, "Ring any bells? Oh, no, my dear. No bells. Are you hearing things? Poor dear. Maybe you should lie down." *Sigh.*

Sea Monster

This Monster was of so huge a size, that coming out of the water, its head reached as high as the masthead; its body was bulky as the ship, and three or four times as long. It had a long pointed snout . . . great broad paws, and the body seemed covered with shell-work, its skin very rugged and uneven.

HANS EGEDE, GREENLAND, 1734 CE

The first official sea-monster sighting was recorded by King Sargon II of Assyria in the year 750 BCE. (He's the same guy whose palace had the carving of the mer-dude, Oannes.) Since then, sea monsters are probably the most common type of mythical creature to be seen. It seems like they're spotted everywhere.

This is a real sea-monster sighting. How cool.

29

This old map shows the waters around Northern Europe. It was drawn by a guy named Olaus Magnus, who lived from 1490 to 1557 CE. He was one of the first mapmakers.

The Gloucester Sea Serpent

It's so cool that we have our very own sea serpent in Massachusetts. (Not that I'll be let out of this town anytime soon to even see the ocean, much less a sea serpent.) Over the last 300 years, there were so many hundreds of sightings of the Gloucester serpent that scientists took notice. No one was ever able to catch it though, and there is still no reliable proof it existed.

"His head was elevated from three to five feet; the distance was about six feet from his neck to the first bunch; we counted twenty bunches, and we supposed them on an average of about five feet apart, and his whole length could not be less than 120 feet . . ."

TIMOTHY HODGKINS, GLOUCESTER, MA, AUGUST 12, 1818 CE

SPECIES OF SEA MONSTERS

Here are my really bad drawings, along with descriptions of Mr. Heuvelmans's unexplained sea monsters.

Heaps of Humps
Size: 60–100 feet
Color: Brown or black with a white underbelly
Skin: Smooth

Slithering Steed
Size: 30–60 feet
Color: Brown, gray, or black
Skin: Smooth and shiny, with short fur like a seal

3

Extraordinary Eel

Size: About 30 feet
Color: Blackish brown or blue back, white underbelly
Skin: Smooth, with fins

4

Periscopic Projector

Size: 15–65 feet
Color: Dark brown, mottled back, yellowish belly
Skin: Rough and wrinkly

Help!

Fantabulous Fins
Size: 60–70 feet
Color: Brown, with yellow patches
Skin: Smooth, but with large plates, like an armadillo

Outlandish Otter
Size: About the size of a whale
Color: Grayish brown
Skin: Rough and wrinkly, like a walrus

My incredibly BRILLIANT {but not very scientific} IDEAS

SEA MONSTERS COULD IN FACT BE:

1 The Kracken

Over thousands of years, there had been so many sightings of a giant tentacled creature, scientists couldn't brush it off as imaginary. They finally discovered the giant squid in the mid 1850s. It's a known fact that giant squids fight with whales. So if you think about it, from underwater, the bottom of a sailing ship might look similar to a whale, yes?

This picture shows scars on the skin of a whale created by the tentacle suckers of a squid. On a normal squid, each sucker is about an inch around. On a giant squid, each one measures about 4 inches around. But some old whaler guys claim to have seen scars that were 24 inches around!

Mistaken Identity

When I found this photo in Ninny's journal, I thought for sure it was the spine and skull of a sea monster. But believe it or not, it's a beached shipwreck on the island of Guam. The frame of the old boat is sticking up out of the sand!

Escaped Circus Elephants

No self-respecting sea monster researcher could forget to mention Nessie, the Loch Ness Monster. There's still no concrete evidence to prove she exists, but there are hundreds of books and movies about her.

It's been rumored that a circus elephant might have escaped and gone for a swim in Loch Ness.

If you look at the parts of the elephant that show above the water, they do look suspiciously like the head and humps of a sea monster. This is a good theory to explain the photo, but it doesn't explain the hundreds of other Nessie sightings.

35

Friday, oct. 28 {4:30 pm}

I finished sea monsters this week, along with studying for tests in almost every subject—the quarter finishes next week. No more Britney as my lab partner! Yay!

Charley has been out sick since Wednesday. He thinks he's developing an allergy to mold. It must be serious, because he hates missing tests. In his absence, I've been faced with the loser-with-no-friends seating dilemma at lunch. Today I found a half-empty table at the back of the cafeteria with some seventh graders. Then the creep and his minions showed up. They sat down, evil oozing from their pores. Kane said, "Hey, Abigail, are you ready for Halloween? Your Princess of Darkness costume is looking good." I just glared at him. Then he said, "But I think you're missing your prince!" He pulled out a flattened roadkill frog and threw it on top of my macaroni and cheese. So that was it for my lunch. I left the cafeteria for my hiding spot in the library.

On the unexpected side, Deke Stoltz talked to me today. I don't know if it's good or bad. All week in English class, I've been ever-so-discreetly watching him doodle in his notebook while Mrs. Beasley acted out scenes from *Romeo and Juliet*. I was hoping to pick up some drawing tips without him noticing. I must not be very good at the discreet thing, because after class he plopped his notebook down on my desk and said, "Yo, you can look at it. Just give it back to me in algebra."

Oh, Romeo, Romeo!

Mrs. Beasley makes a creepy Juliet.

Was he being nice, or was he just sick of me lurking? I was so embarrassed. My face ignited from within and my left armpit started its sprinkler action.

I kept the notebook through biology, lunch, and history. Looking at his class notes and drawings felt strange—so personal. Is that weird? I didn't know how to give it back to him without saying something, so I got to algebra early, left it on his desk with a note that said "Thanks," and kept my head down for the whole class. Ugh.

Saturday, oct. 29 {2:00pm}

For some strange reason, Pop has decided he needs to check on me in my room every now and then. As if I'd be anywhere else. It's annoying! I have to keep all my notes and pages really organized, so if he decides to poke his head in the door, I can cover everything up really fast. Peanut's pretty good about letting me know if someone is coming, so that helps.

Anyway, my latest discovery is that I can order books from the library on the Internet. Why did Charley not tell me this? Instead of having to go to the library, risking the wrath of Pop, I can browse conveniently from my room and pick up books on my way home from school. I know, I sound like a TV commercial.

Today I've been looking for information about the giant spider. I'd never heard of a Tsuchigumo, so I searched the Internet first. I even searched different word combinations like "Japanese spider," and "giant spider." There are no books about it anywhere. But Charley remembered he had a book of Japanese fairy tales with a story about a "goblin spider." That's just about all I could find.

I should also note that it's been over two weeks since this all started and nothing terrible has happened . . .

. . . yet! (Cue music of doom.) But really, maybe nothing will happen. Maybe it's all a joke, or this DF person changed his mind or something.

During the daytime, they look just like common spiders; but very late at night, when everybody is asleep, and there is no sound, they become very, very big, and do awful things.

LAFCADIO HEARN, **THE GOBLIN SPIDER**, 1865 CE

Tsuchigumo was the name of a race of people in ancient Japan who rebelled against the emperor. The emperor's army drove them into the mountains, where legend says they turned into monstrous flesh-eating spiders. They hid in caves and deserted castles, waiting for unsuspecting travelers. After the travelers fell asleep, the spiders wrapped them up to eat them later. Sometimes the spiders changed into human form to lure their prey into their webs.

The only way to escape the spider's web is with a magic spell. No magic? No luck!

Are they real?
Information about the Tsuchigumo was very hard to find, especially since I'm stuck in this town and don't speak Japanese.

Mwa-ha-ha-ha! Wouldn't it be so cool if I had a big pet spider that would eat Kane?

Sunday, oct. 30 {7:00pm}

Tomorrow is Halloween. My least favorite holiday—perhaps my least favorite day—of the whole year. It just serves to emphasize the desolate nature of my young life. Everyone is outside running around, collecting gobs of candy, while I sit here and watch atop piles of dog fur, a forgotten ghost. (That's very poetic, isn't it?)

Monday, oct. 31 {6:00pm}

Halloween mayhem is in full swing. Charley feels better, so he's out trick-or-treating with the Band Geeks. I'm happy for him. Really. He's going to give me all his candy because he's allergic to most of it.

Aside from feeling like a lonely geek, I should probably explain the big reason I hate this day. Both of my parents died on Halloween—two years apart. Isn't that eerie? Maybe there's a Thaddeus Halloween Curse. Maybe that means I'm going to die on Halloween, too. What an uplifting thought.

Anyway, first my mother died. Something went wrong after I was born and she got really sick. Then, two years later, there was a fire here and my father was killed. That's all I know. I've tried asking Ninny and Pop more, but Ninny gets all weepy and rambles nonsense and Pop says I ask too many questions, just like my father.

I found a newspaper clipping in Ninny's bedside stand a long time ago. (I used to snoop around the house a lot when I was younger, pretending to be a detective.) The article was very cryptic. It said the fire started in an upstairs room, but doesn't mention any deaths.

We don't even have any pictures of my parents. Pop got rid of all their stuff because he doesn't want to remember. Didn't he stop to think that I might want to know who they were? The little things: Like did either of them have a sweet tooth? Were either of them socially inept teenagers? If I knew even a few of those things, I might be able to construct an image of my life if they hadn't died. But I have nothing to base anything on.

Actually, I have one thing—a necklace of my mother's. Ninny saved it. She said it was very special and to keep it safe, so I don't wear it. But I do take it out and hold it sometimes. It's always warm. And this is really silly, but ever since I was little, I've imagined that my mother is trying to send me a message through it. If I could only figure out how to receive the message, I could talk to my mom. Yeah, silly. But nobody has to know, right?

So that's enough emotional stuff for today. I'm going to put my spider pages together now.

Orange, yellow, white
So much sugary goodness
In such a small bite.

HAIKU

I await candy delivery
from Charley . . .

Wednesday, Nov. 2 {3:45pm}

Remember the other day when I said it's been over two weeks and nothing has happened yet? I spoke too soon. Ninny couldn't find her shoes, so she asked me to walk down the driveway to get the mail. This letter was in the mailbox.

What the heck is this Board of Mystical Management? How do they know what I'm doing?

Later {5:30pm}

Charley and I tried to imagine what "grave" consequences could mean. The list was too long and scary. We decided to focus on what my options are instead.

Option 1: Tell Pop everything. Get in huge trouble for not telling him sooner. No more BoMM. No more mystery. No more life. Get locked in bedroom for eternity.

Option 2: Don't tell Pop. Stop all research and ignore future feline deliveries. This means no more BoMM. No more mystery. No getting in trouble. Continue boring life.

Option 3: Don't tell Pop. Don't stop research. Mystery continues. Grave consequences loom like dark cloud.

Why do I think that if I choose Option 1 or 2, that won't be the end of it? My DF wants me to find information. The BoMM doesn't want me to find it. And Pop wants to keep everything locked up, including me. Since something is going on anyway, wouldn't I be better off knowing as much as possible? I thought knowledge was supposed to be the best defense. That leaves Option 3.

Even Later {7:30pm}

I'm writing a note to my DF to tell him about everything: the BoMM letter, my research so far, and all the things that are *not* as they seem.

Help!

42

(Cue music of doom.) ♩♩♫♩♩

LETTER OF DOOM!

October 30

Dear Ms. Thaddeus,

It has been brought to our attention that you are delving into matters that do not concern you. Questioning the traditional interpretation of mystical matters is best left to experienced individuals.

We strongly suggest that you cease your endeavors at once. Should you choose to ignore this request, the consequences could be very grave indeed.

Be mindful of our warnings.

Respectfully,

The Board

THE BOARD OF MYSTICAL MANAGEMENT

Thursday, Nov. 3 {4:15pm}

Before yesterday's BoMM letter, I had ordered a bunch of dragon books from the library. Since I've decided to forge ahead with Option 3, I picked them up today. Miss Malkin gave me a really creepy smile today, along with the eyebrow-raising thing.

The most dreaded assignment reared its dragon-like head in history class: the oral report. Ugh. Out of anything in school, standing in front of the class is the absolute worst torture that could be inflicted upon me. It sends me back to first grade when I got picked to read a poem at an assembly. As soon as I got out on the stage, I puked. Everywhere. Since that fateful day, every single time I've had to stand in front of the class, Kane makes gagging noises.

On the home front, Ninny is celebrating Sweet Potato Awareness Month. Her *Potato Magic Cookbook* arrived from the TV shopping channel. This week, I've eaten pancakes, oatmeal, meatloaf, soup, and casserole, all with sweet potato mashed into them.

It's all because of that darn calendar Pop gives her every year. It lists every single holiday and observance known to mankind. In some cases—like National Chocolate Cupcake Day—it's a good thing. But yesterday was Plan Your Epitaph Day. Ninny made me write my epitaph. Ugh. She said, "You can never be too prepared, my dear!" So this is what I wrote. "Abigail Thaddeus, died on Halloween, from a grave consequence."

Oh, report cards were delivered this week. I got two As and four Bs. Not too bad, considering all the teachers took points off my grades for "lack of participation." Pop was happy about that. Not. I need a snack.

Friday, Nov. 4 {3:30 pm}

The cat made an appearance this morning, so I attached my note and off it went. If you told me a month ago I'd be giving notes to a cat, I'd say you were insane.

I should probably start working on my oral report this weekend. It's due a week from Monday. I have to pretend I'm Thomas Jefferson and tell the class why I'm in favor of independence from England. I'd much rather peel off my eyelids.

Saturday, Nov. 5 {9:30 am}

It's cold and rainy outside. Ninny says it might even snow. Today's plan: snuggle with Peanut and read about dragons.

Sunday, Nov. 6 {7:30 am}

Today's plan: Dragons, dragons, and more dragons—but first, I'm going to sneak a bowl of cereal before Ninny tries to feed me a sweet potato something-or-other.

Later {2:30 pm}

Wow, who knew there was so much information on dragons? I went through five books and I don't even know how many websites. But I kept better track of my research this time, so I think I can do the pages this week.

Even Later {10:30 pm}

Signing off for tonight as I eagerly await a reply from my DF. I wonder how long it will take? Or if he'll even write back? If it's a he. Maybe it's a she? I hope it's not an "it."

What if "it" is an alien?

45

Dragon

> Among all the kindes of serpents, there is none comparable to the dragon.
>
> **EDWARD TOPSELL, 1658 CE**

The first dragons were really big snakes. One of the oldest is the ourobouros. Some myths say it was the very first creature in the universe. It would swallow itself by its tail and then be reborn.

This is the hydra, from Greek mythology. If you cut off a head, two new ones will grow in its place. Hercules discovered that if you burn the hole where the head was, no new ones will grow. Good to know in case I run into any hydras.

A DRAGON HAIKU

Mist-covered mountains,
Loom low on the horizon,
Sleeping dragons lie.

I wrote this in English class today. Beasts are showing up in my homework . . . Am I officially obsessed?

DRAGON EVOLUTION

6000 BCE
Rock art in Australia shows the oldest dragon image, the rainbow serpent.

800–338 BCE
The Greeks coin the early term for dragon: *drakonta*. It means "keen vision."

6000 BCE   **5000 BCE**   **4000 BCE**   **3000 BCE**   2 E

2650 BCE
In Egypt's Old Kingdom, the god Denwen is a fire-breathing serpent.

379 CE
In the last days of Roman rule in Europe, Roman soldiers brought the dragon to England in the form of a wind sock flag.

700 CE
In the great epic story of *Beowulf*, the dragon appears for the first time as a treasure-hoarding monster.

1669 CE
One of the last recorded dragon sightings is in Henham, England. It's a timid 9-foot-long amphithere.

circa 1700 CE
No one really believes that dragons are real anymore. Maybe they were hunted to extinction.

Mine!

R.I.P. DRAGONS

1000 BCE

0

1000 CE

2000 CE

1100–1340 CE
The Middle Ages in Europe are a time of great dragon activity. Pictures of the wyvern start to appear. Tales of saints killing dragons are very popular.

circa 1400 CE
Dragons grow two more legs and become the heraldic dragon— the most familiar dragon image.

49

CHINESE DRAGONS

Chinese dragons were pretty nice guys, godlike even, trying to help out poor pathetic humans whenever they could. Some ruled over the weather and brought rain, some protected the palaces of the gods, and some guarded hidden treasure.

They lived for thousands of years. Young dragons would have to swim around for about one thousand years before they could sprout legs and horns. Then after another couple thousand years, they could grow wings. But they didn't use wings to fly. Flying powers came from a bump on the top of their head. Go figure.

Fish could become dragons if they trained really hard and jumped the famous Dragon Gate waterfall on the Yellow River. I guess fish can have dreams too . . .

Lung is the common name for the Chinese dragon. It actually means "deaf." Dragons had ears, but they couldn't hear until they grew horns.

Many dragons carried a pearl of wisdom under their chin. Some people say it's actually a ball of dragon spit. Ew.

The Dragon Stone

A dragon stone is a bright red stone on the forehead of a dragon. You'll be blessed with good luck if you manage to snatch one from a living dragon. If the dragon dies, the stone will turn black and be useless. Seems to me, you'd need the luck BEFORE you tried to snatch the stone.

Dragon Scales

Dragon scales are indestructible. That makes dragons very hard to kill. Should you ever need to slay a dragon, the weakest areas of its body are the throat and belly.

You can use the scales to make a suit of armor!

Dragon's Blood

Dragon's blood is totally poisonous. One drop would kill you instantly. BUT if it's mixed with honey and oil, it can cure blindness and deafness.

My incredibly BRILLIANT {but not very scientific} IDEAS

DRAGONS COULD IN FACT BE:

1

Dinosaur Fossils

People around the world have been discovering fossils for thousands of years. If you dug up dinosaur bones and didn't know what they were, it would be pretty easy to imagine that they came from a dragon. Dinosaurs are like the next best thing to a dragon.

2

An Undiscovered Species

Sightings of the mokele-mbembe in central Africa have been reported for hundreds of years. Local pygmy tribesmen describe the creature as about the size of an elephant, with a long neck and small head. It will attack and kill hippopotamuses and humans, but only eats plants.

Friday, Nov. 11 {7:30pm}

Dragons are done! Yay! But on the downside, I've been so obsessed with my research that I forgot to do an English essay. Ugh. Mrs. Beasley gave me a look and asked if everything was okay at home. My teachers all know about Ninny.

When I was in grade school, Ninny did all kinds of crazy things—like show up at my classroom door shrieking, "Abigail, the wizards are coming to tea! You must come home and help me!" You can imagine my social misery after those episodes.

My left armpit started in as Mrs. Beasley questioned me, but I managed to mumble that everything was fine and that I had just forgotten about the assignment. If I hand it in Monday, I won't get points off. Whew.

So this weekend: essay and oral report. Going to need snacks. Popcorn might do the trick.

Charley said he's got some ideas to help me overcome my public-speaking problems. His social calendar is miraculously open tonight, so he's coming over to watch TV. Charley's grandparents don't believe in TV. With Pop being the control freak he is, I'm surprised we have one—with cable even! Maybe Pop feels guilty for cutting me off from the rest of human civilization. That, and Ninny would be lost without the TV shopping channel.

No feline deliveries yet. No suspicious BoMM activity.

Saturday, Nov. 12 {11:00am}

Pop did his prison-guard check early today, so I figured it was safe for me to sneak around in The Room for a little while. In one of Ninny's journals, I found some notes about Australia. What a strange coincidence given that the bunyip is my next creature.

HAIKU

Kernels in the pan,
Pop with reckless abandon,
Then drown in butter.

I didn't find any information about the bunyip in there, but Ninny's notes did say she found a present for my mother—a necklace with two powerful opal stones, one white and one black. This little poem was stuck on the page:

O mighty stone of fiery white,
Strengthen the mind
with power of light.
O mighty stone of fiery black,
Strengthen the body
to stand attack.

Wow. What if my mother's necklace really does have magical powers?

Sunday, Nov. 13 {4:00 pm}

I ate way too much popcorn today. But it got me through the English essay, the bunyip, and Thomas Jefferson. Now for Charley's oral report wisdom. . . .

Later {7:30 pm}

Charley's instructions: First, inhale deeply. Imagine my breath flowing down my legs, into the ground, planting me like a tree. (A mobile tree, or I won't be able to walk back to my seat.) Next, imagine everyone in their underwear. Then imagine my vocal cords plugged into my brain, like speakers, with the activation switch being my left earlobe. Last, memorize my notecards. Repeat them out loud, in my room, a hundred times, so I don't have to think about what I'm actually saying.

His strategy is to overload my brain with new tasks, bypassing my normal panic mode. Right. It sounds confusing to me. Stay tuned for the next episode of "As Abigail's Stomach Turns."

Bunyip

How can you be afraid of something called a bunyip? It sounds like a cute little pet!

But it's not! The original tribal people of Australia (Aborigines) had so many different descriptions for the bunyip, it's hard to say what it looks like. It is most commonly described as having flippers, tusks, scales, and long dark hair, and it is about the size of a large dog.

AND IT'S REALLY EVIL.

Like the kill-you-on-the-spot-and-eat-you kind of evil.

THE CHALLICUM BUNYIP

Scale 1 pace to ¾ inch.
Figure 11 paces long

From this side, it looks like a seal.

From this side, it looks like a whale.

Sketch of a figure of the "Bunyip" cut by the aborigines in the turp on the bank of a on from Challicum station, near Ararat, Victoria. Sketch taken by Mr. J. H. Scott mvean about June 1867.

This picture shows the outline of a bunyip. It was drawn by a man named Reynell Eveleigh Johns in 1856 CE. He said that each year, a tribe of Aborigines recut this shape into the bank of a creek. It's the outline of a dead bunyip. It was called the Challicum Bunyip after the town nearby.

Monday, Nov. 14 {4:30pm}

Here's today's exciting episode of "As Abigail's Stomach Turns." Being that history class is after lunch, I was a bit worried about the whole puking possibility, so I decided to hang out in the library instead of eating lunch.

In class I tried to stay calm by zoning out during everyone else's reports. When Mr. Jellyhob called my name, I took a deep breath and imagined the whole tree-root thing. Then I totally forgot the rest of what Charley told me to do. My thoughts were racing around like crazy. I walked up to the front of the room with Kane's gagging noises in the background, then turned around. All of a sudden, it was like the whole class got sucked into a little black tube. The next thing I remember was hearing Mr. Jellyhob: "Abigail, Abigail, wake up, dear. Oh, my, someone get the nurse!" I opened my eyes to his big pink face hanging over mine. My head was throbbing. When I realized I'd fainted, I was horrified. Everyone in the room was in silent shock. Then Charley popped up and offered to get a wheelchair to wheel me down to the nurse's office.

Apparently, as I was fainting I said, "I'm Jhomas Tefferson . . . pretty purple dots . . . underwear" and that was it. I'm toast. The nurse called Pop to pick me up, which he was not thrilled about after she told him that I hadn't eaten anything all day. I should *not* have given her that confession. All the way home, Pop lectured me about being responsible for my personal well-being.

Today ranks a close second to the day last year when the Britneys wrote "Abigail loves Kane" all over my locker in black Magic Marker.

Tuesday, Nov. 15 {4:30 pm}

This morning in English class, Deke Stoltz talked to me again. As soon as he said, "Yo, Ab," I braced myself for a remark about yesterday's disaster, but he pointed to my notebook and said, "Some pretty cool dragons there." I couldn't believe that he actually liked my silly doodles—or that he would even talk to me after yesterday.

In other news, my research is now turning to bats. I think I'm procrastinating though. I don't want to know if there's even the slightest possibility of giant bats existing somewhere.

In case I haven't made it clear, I have an extreme dislike of bats. Since I was little, I've had a knack for stray bat encounters. They've landed in my hair more than once, and it always freaks me out. Apparently, it's very unusual for a bat to do that. Why don't FUN unusual things happen to me instead? So now I have unrealistic fears of being bitten by a rabid bat in the night and dying a horrible death. On Halloween.

Later {7:30 pm}

Okay, homework is done. Time for giant bats.

Wednesday, Nov. 16 {7:00 pm}

I found out one of the reasons why it's so hard to prove that mythical beasts exist: the places where they're rumored to live, like Java, home of the ahool, are really far away from modern civilization. Some places don't even have roads. Imagine scientists trekking through a jungle or over steep mountains or across a desert, lugging tons of equipment like video cameras and recording devices. Ugh. Challenging, to say the least.

A GIANT BAT, NAMED FOR ITS CRY

To the people who live in Java, the ahool isn't mythical at all. It's real. Very real!

The ahool has the face of a monkey and a dark gray, furry body about the same size as a one-year-old child. Its wingspan is about 12 feet across—as big as a car! It's been seen hunting at night, gliding along the surface of rivers, scooping up fish with its feet.

Most bats have terrible vision. They "see" by sending out high-pitched sounds that bounce off objects around them. The echoes from their calls tell them where to fly. It's called echolocation.

This isn't a bat, it's a pterosaur. But it does look a bit like a bat with no fur, doesn't it?

Java is a remote, rain forest-covered island near Australia.

This is a drawing of pterodactyls, as imagined by English naturalist Edward Newman in 1843 CE. They look like flying rats.

JAVA ISN'T THE ONLY HOME OF GIANT BATS

The kongamato is red, with a 4–7 foot wingspan and a face like a dog. It lives in various regions of Africa. When trying to describe it, local people have pointed to pictures of pterosaurs.

61

Saturday, Nov. 19 {8:30am}

Did I mention that I hate bats? Oh, silly me, of course I did. But I'll say it again. *I hate bats!*

Bat Incident No. 2: This time the bat got into my room, even though my door was closed. This bat was bigger, blacker, and swoopier than the first. Peanut went crazy. Pop couldn't catch it. It flew up toward the attic and disappeared. Ninny shrieked, "Spy!" Pop yelled at me to get back to bed and then disappeared into the attic himself for almost an hour. I wish the bats would just go away!

Anyway, we're heading out to MegaMart soon, thank goodness. My snack stash ran out, so I tore apart my room and found an old package of cookies from last summer. I had to pick out dog fur, but they didn't taste half bad. When they ran out, I had to resort to my fingernails.

My fingers are now bloody stumps.

Later {1:30pm}

The MegaMart mission was a success. My snack stash is replenished, and Ninny's Thanksgiving dinner shopping is complete. I was able to distract her as she passed the sweet potatoes.

So I guess I need to catch up here. Let's see. Word about my fainting incident spread pretty quickly. All week long there were giggles, snickers, and pointing everywhere I turned. My left armpit was on overdrive. In every class Kane pretended to faint while his minions tried fake revival techniques. At least I got a B on the report. Mr. Jellyhob just graded my notecards. He's been super nice to me. I don't think he wanted to risk another fainting episode. Maybe he thinks I have a fatal disease.

We got assigned new lab partners this week. We have an odd number of kids in the class, so Mrs. Badger said I could join a group or do the work on my own. I decided to go it alone. Charley is now paired up with Britney #1. Nightmare. He's delirious. He's all gaga and thinks she likes him! She's all, "Oh, Charley, I'm SO glad you're my lab partner. Why haven't we ever been partners before?" She just wants him to do her work, and he's totally clueless—he thinks his plan to become popular is working.

He's marching with the band at the football game today. I wonder how it's going. It's been cold and rainy all week, and he's been completely paranoid about getting sick. His parents are coming to visit at Thanksgiving and have promised to take him to New York City for the weekend. If he misses the trip because he's sick again, he'll freak. His dad is always telling him to toughen up. I think he wants to prove he's not a wimp. He's been drinking loads of that algae stuff, doing steam baths, taking vitamin C, and wearing antibacterial hand gel clipped to his belt loop.

Britney is SO annoying!

Sunday, Nov. 20 {11:00am}

Working on gryphons today. Even though the oldest images of gryphons date back about 5,000 years, there aren't any recorded sightings of them, ever. Maybe because they lived in the faraway northern mountains of Europe? That would put them into the hard-to-get-to category, like the ahool. And since they supposedly eat people, maybe no one lived to tell once they saw one.

I'd like to get these pages done today. Then I have to study for another algebra quiz. Mr. Billow is quiz happy.

No sign of the cat this week.

Gryphon

I found this ancient Roman coin with a gryphon on it!

The griffin is both a feathered animal and a quadruped; its body is like that of a lion, but it has wings and the face of an eagle.

ISIDORE OF SEVILLE, ETYMOLOGIES, 600 CE

If you met a gryphon, it would most likely eat you. Apparently, they're not fond of people, except as food. People try to steal their gold. And gryphons LOVE gold. Emeralds, too.

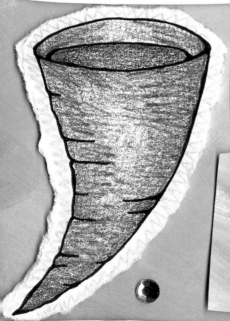

FEATHER OF TRUTH

The owner of a gryphon feather can make someone tell the truth.

CLAW OF PURITY

When used as a cup, the gryphon's claw will change color if the drink is poisoned.

The ancient Greeks said that gryphons lived in the northern mountains of Europe, where they battled with one-eyed giants—the Arimaspeans—who tried to steal their gold.

So this is why that sultan guy died! He thought he had a gryphon claw that would detect poison in his drink!

Monday, Nov. 21 {7:20 pm}

Today in school, Charley wore a surgical mask to shield himself from germs. Kane teased him, of course, but Britney batted her eyelashes at Charley and said, "Stop making fun. I think it makes him look mysterious." Ugh.

I need some books about the phoenix to read over the long weekend. Pickings are slim at our little library, and I don't want to wait a week to have them delivered from other libraries. Maybe Charley and I can sneak down the street to Bilbo's Books—if Charley's grandmother will cover for us again. I've been stashing away extra lunch money from Ninny's jar for just such an excursion.

Still no kitty. Things are too quiet.

Tuesday, Nov. 22 {6:40 pm}

Covert Bookstore Operation No. 1 went well. I told Pop I needed to go to Charley's to work on a project. I really hate lying, but technically that was true—just not *totally* true. Charley's grandmother was easy. One compliment about her new fluffy scarf and she was all aflutter.

They had some good stuff at the store. I found three books: *Wonder Beasts*, *Fabulous Beasts*, and *Willy Ley's Exotic Zoology*. They all have chapters on the phoenix.

At first I was slightly creeped out by the girl working there. She had purple hair, black eyeliner, and a ring in her nose. She was drawing all over her arms with a black marker and said, "Yo, you need help, lemme know," without looking up. When we got to the checkout, she asked, "So, what kinda project are *these* books for? Beasts, hmmm. Don't remember studying this stuff. What grade are you in? Do you guys know my little brother, Deke? He's in eighth grade."

The "Yo" should have given it away for me. And the drawing. Charley told her our names, and she nodded, "Oh yeah, Abigail. Deke mentioned your name the other day." I managed to nod back and smile while my left armpit suddenly activated at the idea that Deke talked about me to his sister. She didn't look at me like, "Oh, THAT girl— the one who can't talk and faints and lurks and stuff." Maybe he didn't say anything bad.

Wednesday, Nov. 23 {8:30pm}

School got out early today, so I've been helping Ninny with Thanksgiving dinner. I like to check to make sure she reads the recipes right and doesn't mess up the ingredients. She's been known to confuse salt and sugar, among other things. And guess what? No sweet potatoes on the menu! She kept asking me if I knew what she was forgetting. I didn't remind her. Mwa-ha-ha-ha!

Thursday, Nov. 24 {8:00pm}

Charley's parents came for Thanksgiving dinner, which was really cool. They're so glamorous. They look like movie stars. Normally we just have Charley and his grandparents, so it was nice to have someone from the outside world. Charley's grandmother wore her gigantic purple feathered hat, which dropped feathers all over the table every time she turned her head. Charley's grandfather is obsessed with baseball and likes to throw food instead of passing it. At least this year he yelled, "Fly ball!" before he tossed me a dinner roll. But for the most part, dinner was uneventful— until dessert.

I was thinking about my research, eating my pie and counting feathers floating between the dishes, when Pop slammed his fist down on the table so hard all the dishes jiggled. Charley's mother said, "But, Alistair, you have to let her out of this house sooner or later! She needs to be prepared for life!" I guessed they were talking about me.

Pop looked like he was going to explode. "This is none of your business, Chloe! This is my house, my rules, and my grandchild. I'll thank you to remember that." He got up from the table and disappeared down the basement stairs.

We all finished our pie in silence.

Charley told me after dinner that his mom had been pressing Pop to let me go to New York with them this weekend. He didn't want to get my hopes up, so he didn't tell me. I'm glad he didn't tell me. My despair would only be that much deeper if I had known ahead of time. *Sigh.* Will I ever get out of this town? At least Charley gets to go somewhere. I'm glad he didn't get sick. Really. And I'm not being sarcastic. It's got to be tough having parents that you don't get to see very often.

Flaky buttery
Crust filled with juicy apples,
Dripping cinnamon.

HAIKU

Sunday, November 27 {9:30am}

There is SO MUCH information on the phoenix. I've been gathering information all weekend, trying to forget the fact that I *could* be in New York, if it wasn't for my prison-guard grandfather. My goal is to finish collecting all my notes today so I can work on putting the pages together during the week.

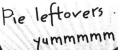

Pie leftovers . . .
yummmmm

Monday, Dec. 5 {4:20pm}

FINALLY!!! The cat delivered another note today. Except it doesn't make me feel any better. All I have now are more questions. Who's hiding the truth? What lies ahead? And the biggie—what impending catastrophe might drive me to exercise heroic efforts?

{ANOTHER NOTE!}

```
Dearest Abigail,

I received your note. Know this: there
are those who hide the truth, who wish
to keep it for themselves. Do not stop
your research. This knowledge will be
necessary for what lies ahead.

You are more special than you know,
Abigail. Your future holds much. But
be careful whom you trust. Stay safe.
Do not exercise heroic efforts.

Sincerely,
Your Devoted Friend
```

I'm in the same spot I was in before I got this note—risking safety from some unknown danger to learn about mythical beasts. Like I said before, even if I did stop now, there's something weird going on here and I'd rather know as much as I can. What if I have some secret destiny like all those orphans in literature? Okay, maybe that's over the top. But this note says I'm special. . . . What if it's true?

Wednesday, Dec. 7 {6:30am}

Another strange incident to report. This shall be known as the "Unknown-Noise-Outside-My-Window Incident." In the middle of the night I awoke to the strangest animal sound I've ever heard. Actually, Peanut heard it first and woke me up with his whining. It started close to my window, faded away, then came back again. The sound was a cross between a screech and a howl. Whatever the animal was, it was big, and it was flying.

I couldn't sleep after that, so I decided to search online for whatever made that sound. Charley was online—he heard the sound from his house, too. We searched through sound clips of owls, hawks, eagles, and every other large bird we could think of. No matches. Creepy.

Creature of doom!

Later {7:45pm}

Working on the phoenix pages tonight. My homework load is light because tomorrow we have a field trip to a community theater to see the play *A Christmas Carol*.

I really like plays, and I love getting out of Westbrook, even if it's only two towns over. But I could really do without the whole social aspect of school field trips. Especially since Pop decided to chaperone. Ugh. What's with his sudden need to be involved? It wouldn't be so bad if he wasn't, well, for lack of a better word, so Pop-like—all straightlaced and stone-faced. I'm not sure what he's trying to do. Unless it's just another way for him to keep tabs on me. Well, maybe he'll pay attention to the play and take a lesson from Mr. Scrooge.

Humbug!

Thursday, Dec. 8 {4:45pm}

On the bus ride Pop intimidated the whole class into silence. He wasn't going out of his way to be menacing or anything. In fact, I think he might have even been trying to put on a grandfatherly sort of face. (I only know this because I know what his normal everyday face looks like.) But he just exudes his Pop vibe no matter what. I'm sure the teachers loved the silent ride. They'll probably invite him back for every single field trip until I graduate. Ugh.

During the play, the Britneys sat behind Charley and me. They kept teasing him, kicking his seat, saying, "He's so cute!" in annoying girly voices. I wanted to puke, but Charley ate it right up. Poor Charley. They're laughing behind his back; I know it. I don't want to burst his happy little bubble, but I don't know how much longer I can let him go on believing that Britney #1 likes him.

Friday, Dec. 9 {9:30pm}

I didn't think it was possible to be more humiliated than I was by the fainting spell. What could be worse than that, you ask? How about getting my journal STOLEN—by none other than the creep?

Outside biology class today, Kane did the accidental-bumping-into-me thing, knocking my books all over the place. He spied my journal right away; it looks a little unusual. "Oooh, what do we have here?" He opened it, and said, "It's the innermost thoughts of Abigail Thaddeus!" I was frantic—flailing around, trying to grab it from him. But he tossed it to his minions. The bell rang and they took off. I panicked and both armpits went into overdrive. My journal was in the hands of the enemy. And next period was lunch! I was headed for certain doom.

Part of me wanted to hide out in the library for the rest of the day. But the other part of me was furious. I wanted to march into the lunchroom and take my journal back by force.

Then Charley ran up, all out of breath, because he saw Kane with my journal. The implications of this despicable act started to sink in. Not only was there the potential for the whole school to know my innermost thoughts, but my research would be right out there for everyone to see. According to my DF, it's supposed to be secret. What happens if it's not? Not to mention losing all those hours of typing and cutting and pasting and drawing. It's ME in those pages! (And cookie crumbs and dog fur.)

We got into the lunchroom and saw that Kane, his minions, the Britneys, and the Jock camp were sitting at the back tables. They all leaned in toward something at the center of the table—my journal. Britney #4 looked up, saw us, and made a throat-clearing noise. Everyone sat down.

I had to fortify myself. I had to prepare myself to actually *say* something, and with authority, no less. I took a deep breath. I did Charley's tree-visualization thing. I was so nervous, but Charley kept whispering that he knew I could do it. I got up to the table, stood behind Kane and forced the words out of my mouth. It was like trying to talk underwater, but I did it.

"Give me back my journal," I said. Kane pretended like he heard a small noise. "What was that?" he asked without turning around. The minions sniggered. "Give it back!" I said, but my voice cracked. Then he said, "I did hear something. I think it was Abigail Thaddeus. She speaks!" I stood there fuming.

I could see something being passed around under the table. Charley asked Britney to give it back, but she played dumb with her hands in the air. "I don't know what you mean, pumpkin."

I pictured Charley and me running around the table, my journal being tossed around in a cruel game of keep-away. How pathetic would that be? I left the lunchroom in defeat.

Why, oh, why did I have to bring my journal to school? I was certain my life was completely over—that my remaining years of school were about to become completely unbearable. Soon Kane and everyone in the eighth grade would know all my secrets.

But then, out of the blue, I was saved. I got to algebra class early, willing myself to become invisible. Deke walked in. He was carrying my journal! He plopped it on my desk. I was speechless—even more than my normal state of speechlessness. He said, "You owe me one." I blurted out a "Thanks," while my face turned pink. "And I didn't read it, so don't worry," he said.

And so I was saved. In algebra class. By Deke Stoltz. My relief was deeper than the oceans. I vowed to never, ever take my journal from the safety of my room.

However, it doesn't change the fact that Kane and everyone saw it. Who knows how much they had time to read.

The rest of my weekend will be devoted to putting the phoenix pages together. If I have time, I'll look for books about my next creatures: the pterippi and the unicorn.

Choir of angels singing for me.

> They have also another sacred bird called the phoenix. . . . Indeed it is a great rarity, even in Egypt, only coming there once in 500 years, when the old phoenix dies.
>
> **HERODOTUS, 400 BCE**

The first person to write about the phoenix was a Greek historian named Herodotus, who lived around 400 BCE. He visited Egypt, where he saw pictures of the phoenix. It looked like an eagle, with feathers of red and gold.

The legend of the phoenix supposedly comes from the Benu bird, the ancient Egyptian bird of the sun. But the Benu bird is a heron. It doesn't match the description above.

The phoenix looks nothing like the Benu bird.

Herodotus's description sounds more like the Egyptian god Horus, doesn't it? I wonder if he got confused.

But the resemblance to Horus is striking!

This is very curious.

75

How DID THE Phoenix GET ITS Flames?

The description of the phoenix wasn't the only thing that confused me. Herodotus also wrote down the story of the phoenix, as it was told to him by the Egyptians. Here it is.

Myrrh is sticky tree sap.

Story No. 1

Once every 500 years, a bird flies from Arabia to Egypt to the temple of the sun in the city of Heliopolis, carrying the body of its dead parent encased in a ball of myrrh.

My first question: But what about the whole "reborn from the flames" thing?

I really wanted to find the answer. So it took some major research, but I found out. The story kept changing, but I followed the trail and eventually came to the fiery phoenix. I have no good explanation for how all these strange elements made their way into the story.

Why did my Dad have to be so heavy?

Hi!

Story No. 2
BY PLINY THE ELDER (23–79 CE)
When it's ready to die, the phoenix builds a nest out of cinnamon sticks and other spicy things. After it dies in the nest, a little worm pops out of the dead body and grows into a new phoenix.

Story No. 3
BY TACITUS (55–120 CE)
Flocks of birds follow the phoenix on its journey to the temple in Egypt. At the temple of the sun, it drops the ball of myrrh into a fire.

Hey guys, a little help here?

Story No. 4
BY LACTANIUS (260–340 CE)
As soon as the phoenix dies in its nest, the heat of the sun makes it burst into flames. The yucky little worm grows again, but this time, it grows into an egg with the baby phoenix inside. Its feathers are every color of the rainbow, and it even has jeweled eyes.

My incredibly BRILLIANT {but not very scientific} IDEAS

THE PHOENIX COULD IN FACT BE:

Ow! Ow! Hot! Hot!

1

Smokey the Crow

Crows do this really weird thing called "passive anting." They will stand on top of an ant's nest and let ants run all over their bodies. The reason for this is most likely because the ants will eat the tiny biting feather mites that hang out on the crow. Crows have also been seen sitting with their wings spread over the embers of a dying fire—probably for the same reason. So picture this: when the bird gets too hot, it flaps its wings to take off, stirring up the dying fire. Ta-da! Bird rising from flames!

Okay, maybe that's a little far-fetched. But it's interesting!

2 An Eclipse

Say you were living a few thousand years ago—no books, no TV, no Internet. (Yeah, bleak existence, I know.) One day, the sun goes dark. You look up to see a black disk with fiery winglike things covering the sun, like in this photo. What would you think? Maybe that a big flaming bird just flew in front of the sun?

Everyone knows you're not supposed to look directly at an eclipse. But photographers have been able to take images like this that show what it might actually look like if you did look at it.

And then if you wanted to record this strange sight, you'd carve it into rock. Maybe it would look like this?

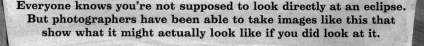

This is a sun disk used in ancient Iran as a symbol for Shamash, god of the sun.

Monday, Dec. 12 {3:30 pm}

As expected, I was Kane's prime target today. A sampling of his witty comments: "I'm the Biggest Creep That Ever Lived? That really hurts," and, "Hey, Abigail, discover any new dragons yet?"

Then, walking past the Britneys, I got, "Yeah girls, too bad we're brainless. But unlike *some* people, *we* have friends." *Sigh.* Surprisingly though, that was all. No other stray comments, no pointing, no whispering, no giggling. I'm highly suspicious.

The phoenix pages took me all weekend, so I didn't look for any new books. I already have books with chapters on unicorns, but nothing about the pterippi. Pegasus, the winged horse, seems to be the most famous example, but I can't find much about any others. Since I had good luck at Bilbo's, maybe I can sneak over there this week. In the meantime, I'm thinking ahead and ordering from the library website for the barometz, barguest, and the bonnacon.

Tuesday, Dec. 13 {8:00 pm}

Covert Bookstore Operation No. 2 was a success. Except I had to go alone. I had hoped Charley's grandmother would let us go again, but after Pop's Thanksgiving explosion, she didn't want to risk upsetting him if he found out. So I climbed out Charley's bedroom window and ran down the street to Bilbo's. I felt like a spy!

Zoey was working. For some reason, I didn't feel quite so tongue-tied around her, but then she asked me if I wanted more books for that journal thing I was working on. *Journal thing?* I must have looked at her like she had three heads. She said, "Yeah, Deke told me that Kane kid swiped your journal, but the kids who saw it thought it was pretty cool."

My tongue began to curl into a knot, but I gave a brilliant reply. Something like, "Oh, yeah, um, it's not really that great." Zoey just shrugged her shoulders and said, "Whatever," and led me over to the mythology section. Then she said, "By the way, that Kane kid? Don't let him get to you. I've been dealing with his older brothers my whole life. They all act like jerks."

So first: Deke said that everyone liked my journal. Wow. And second: Kane has jerky older brothers? That explains a lot.

Anyway, I found two unicorn books that I could afford, but nothing more about the pterippi. I thought winged horses would be more common—like there should be stories about herds of them on the ancient plains of Egypt. I guess I'll have to go with my Pegasus findings.

Thursday, Dec. 15 {12:30am}

Bat Incident No. 3: Another bat! Here I am, minding my own business, finishing my pterippi pages, and Mr. Bat swoops down over my head—one of the swoopy black variety. But Peanut was all over it. He caught it and galloped into Ninny and Pop's bedroom to wake them up. Pop then whisked it up to the attic and stayed up there for over an hour—again. Should I try to find out what's up there? *(Shudder.)*

Friday, Dec. 16 {5:00pm}

Today is National Chocolate-Covered Anything Day. I love chocolate, but I'm afraid of what Ninny's cooking for dinner. She won't let me in the kitchen. It's a surprise.

Note to self: Next year, skip the chocolate-covered chicken.

Pterippi

... OR WINGED HORSE

When Perseus cut off Medusa's head, the blood sinking into the ground produced the winged horse Pegasus.

**THOMAS BULLFINCH,
BULLFINCH'S MYTHOLOGY, 1855**

Pegasus is the most famous winged horse, at least in this part of the world. He carried the Greek hero Bellerophon on his quest to kill the chimera, a terrible monster with a lion's head, a goat's head, and a snake head on its tail.

There are magical flying horses from all over the world: India, Tibet, Thailand, and China. Either they lived with the gods, pulled chariots for the gods, or carried gods and mythical heroes across the skies. No regular people have ever seen one. So I guess I'd have to conclude that they're purely mythical.

I made this! Isn't it cool?

Saturday, Dec. 17 {9:00am}

At 7:00 this morning, Ninny burst into my room with, "Abigail, it's fruitcake weather! Get dressed because we're going shopping!" Ninny and I make fruitcakes every year at the first sign of snow. Finally, snow! I love snow.

Hopefully there'll be time for me to shop for Christmas gifts while we're at MegaMart. (And snacks. Mustn't forget snacks.) Ninny always gives me a little bit of money for Christmas shopping. It feels weird—she's basically giving me money to buy her a present. But she always says, "I love what you pick out for me, dear. That alone is a gift to me." Good old Ninny.

Later {7:30pm}

Whew! We baked twenty-two fruitcakes. They're soaking in brandy before Ninny ships them to faraway relatives I don't know.

For Christmas, I got Pop a fancy pen, like I do every year. I don't know what else to get him. Ninny's gift is a new apron, and Charley is getting a desk calendar with 365 Useless Facts. And I bought some cookies, along with *baked* potato chips. Charley keeps telling me I need healthier snacks.

Speaking of Charley, his parents are coming back for Christmas. He's very excited. They don't often make two trips in a row like this.

Hey, it just started snowing again!

Sunday, Dec. 18 {8:00pm}

No homework, so Charley and I decided to watch holiday movies and eat *baked* potato chips all day. Taking a research break.

HAIKU

Crispy potato,
Sliced into paper-thin rounds.
A delicate crunch.

Fruitcake (of doom).

Tuesday, Dec. 20 {8:00pm}

Pop brought our Christmas tree home today. If it wasn't for the fact that Ninny loves Christmas so much, I'm sure he wouldn't bother. He plunked the tree in the stand and descended to his dungeon.

I asked Ninny what Pop does down there all the time. She stopped for a second and thought. "Well, let's see. I don't remember exactly. He's got hundreds of old radios that he's forever trying to fix." This was nothing she hadn't already told me in the past. I decided to ask her again if she remembered the secret she wanted to tell me. Every once in a while I ask, and this time was no different—she couldn't remember.

Sunday, Dec. 25 {7:00pm}

Ho, ho, ho! Christmas today. Pop was uncharacteristically pleasant this morning as we opened presents. Ninny and Pop both liked their gifts. They gave me a scarf, slippers, a new bathrobe, and ten pairs of socks. Why must every gift-giving opportunity mean new socks? My great aunt Anya sent me a set of Japanese spinning tops. She also sent us a fruitcake—the same kind that Ninny sent her. We had that for breakfast. Then Ninny and I worked on making dinner: roast beef with potatoes, gravy, beans, squash, and pumpkin pie. Yum.

All the Winkleys came for dinner. Charley gave me a miniature Statue of Liberty that he got in New York. It's so cute. He loved the calendar I picked out for him. Oh, and his parents gave him the best gift ever. A real knight's shield! It'll be about fifteen years before he can lift it, but it's totally cool anyway.

There is an ox of the shape of a stag, between whose ears a horn rises from the middle of the forehead, higher and straighter than those horns which are known to us.

JULIUS CAESAR, THE GALLIC WARS, BOOK 6, CHAPTER 26, WRITTEN AROUND 51 BCE

Wow, even the famous Roman emperor Julius Caesar wrote about the unicorn!

A Unicorn shall be caught

on this 12th day of June, if weather shall be favorable.

Whereby we shall bring a maiden of young years and fair face by which she shall be tied to the largest oak in the wood.

Being that the beast will be drawn to the goodness of the maiden, and upon which knee will rest its head, whereby we shall strike.

Men, strong of constitution, are needed. Inquire with Mr. Tobias Johnson.

Unicorns are solitary and aloof. That means they like to be alone. I can't say I blame them. They were hunted down for their horns, which supposedly had magical powers.

I found this clipping in The Room in one of Ninny's travel journals. I wonder where she got it? There was no note; it was just stuck between two pages. What a cruel plan!

The Unicorn's Magical Horn

The unicorn's horn, also called an alicorn, was very special. It could cure diseases, detect poison in food, and purify drinking water. Back in medieval days, the easiest way to kill a powerful dude that you didn't like (without getting caught) was to poison his food. Cups were made from the horns, and powdered horn was a medicine.

THE PRICE TAG

Pieces of horn were worth ten times their weight in gold—whole horns could sell for twice that. Powdered horn wasn't quite as bad—it was only worth three times its weight in gold.

I was curious about how much this little packet would cost in today's dollars. So I weighed the envelope on Pop's postal scale. It weighed 0.75 ounces. Then I looked up the price of gold online. It's $935 per ounce. I think this would be the equation. My math teacher would be so proud.

I found this little envelope in one of Ninny's journals in The Room. She got this at a market in London and was amazed that people were still trying to pass it off as real.

(0.75 oz x $935) 3 = $2103.75

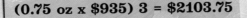

Wow! all that for a packet of powder!

HOW DO YOU KNOW IF IT'S REAL?

Since unicorn horns were so expensive, people wanted to make sure that what they were buying was real. There were several different tests to determine if unicorn horn or powder was authentic. Here are a few.

Test No. 1

Put the horn in a large pot with three scorpions. If the scorpions die within an hour, the horn is real.

No, not in the pot with the unicorn horn!

Test No. 2

Put the horn in milk. If the milk boils and turns brown, then the horn is real.

Test No. 3

Draw a circle on the ground with powdered horn. Put a spider inside the circle. If the spider jumps out of the circle, the horn is real.

Help!

WHAT THEY REALLY WERE

Vikings, from the cold northern oceans, sold horns to European traders, who thought they were from unicorns. They were actually the singular tooth of a rare whale called the narwhal.

That's pretty mean, isn't it? Those poor narwhals.

My incredibly BRILLIANT {but not very scientific} IDEAS

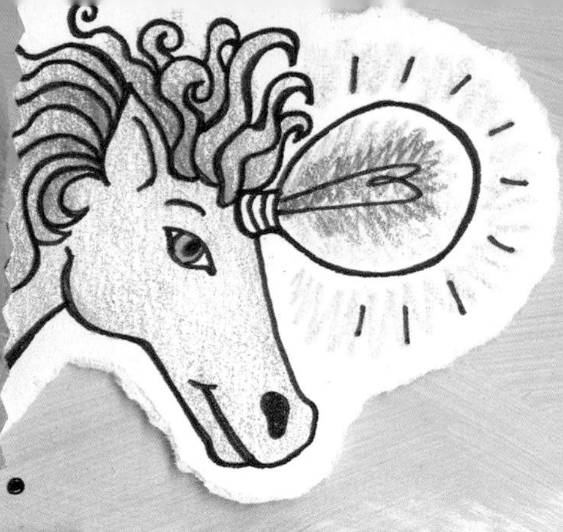

UNICORNS COULD IN FACT BE:

1

Rhinoceroses

The rhino is the only four-legged creature with a single horn on its head. (It's not really a horn. It's made from tons of little hairs all pressed together really tightly.) Tales of the single-horned rhino may have been mistakenly attributed to unicorns.

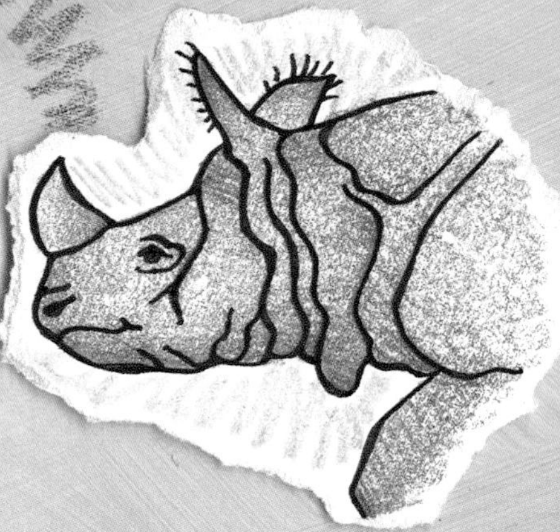

2

Oryxes

Based on all the horse-like descriptions of unicorns, I think it's much more likely that unicorn sightings were of an oryx or an antelope with one horn broken off.

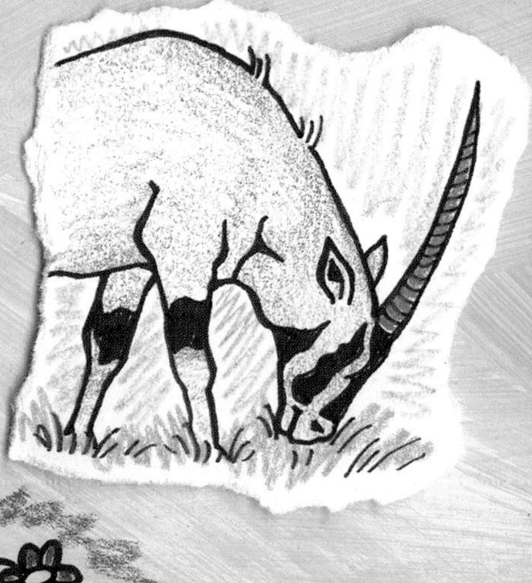

Biologically Engineered

Sheep, goat, and cattle herders in India and Africa learned to make the horns of an animal grow together in the center of its forehead. They either used these animals as the leaders of their herds or gave them away as special gifts. It's entirely possible that travelers might have seen them.

A man named Dr. Franklin Dove created a one-horned cow in 1933. He surgically moved the horn buds on a calf so that they would grow together in the center of its forehead.

I don't know how my inner animal-rights activist feels about manipulating these poor animals. But I guess this means that unicorns can be real.

BULL WITH SINGLE HORN IS MODERN UNICORN

WHAT might be called a modern unicorn has been produced by Dr. W. F. Dove, University of Maine biologist. From a day-old bull calf, Dr. Dove removed the two small knots of tissue which normally develop into horns. These horn buds he transplanted in the center of the bull's forehead, thereby inducing the growth of a single massive horn. The bull, now nearly three years old, has developed much of the proud bearing ascribed to the mythical unicorn.

91

Thursday, Dec. 29 {8:15am}

Woo-hoo! Finished the unicorn last night.

And . . . by some miracle, Pop is letting me go to Boston tomorrow with Charley and his mom! I can't believe it!

Friday, Dec. 30 {10:00pm}

What an amazing, fantastic day. The best day I've ever had. Charley's mom took us to Newbury Street, a fancy shopping area. I felt like I was in a movie. We went to a comic-book store, a music shop, and some funky clothing stores. Then we had lunch at a really nice restaurant. The menu was so fancy, I couldn't tell what half the foods were. Charley's mom ordered a few dishes for us to sample. My favorite was lobster ravioli in saffron cream sauce, and, of course, dessert! Pecan caramel mud slide. Heaven. I will remember this day for the rest of my life.

Saturday, Dec. 31 {10:30am}

Still floating from yesterday. I don't want to jinx myself, but I daresay my life is looking up. I went to a city, visited cool stores, and ate in a restaurant. Deke Stoltz likes my drawings, I seem to be able to actually speak, at least to a few people, and even though my journal was stolen, the kids who saw it apparently liked it. Yes, my dark cloud of doom is still looming, but I'm ignoring it.

Later {2:00pm}

Ninny and Pop left to visit the Winkleys for "New Year's Eve Tea." I can hardly believe my good fortune. They rarely leave me alone, so even though I don't want to, now is a perfect time to find out what's going on with the bats in the attic. (Shudder.) Charley's going to help me break in.

Even Later {5:30 pm}

With a little Internet research, Charley figured out how to pick the attic door lock with a coat hanger. Flashlights in hand, we ventured into the darkness. The first room was filled with old boxes and furniture and a couple of those old dress dummies. (Why do old, creepy attics always have those things?) We made our way to the far end, to the tower door. Guess what we found inside? You got it. Bats. Hundreds of them, hibernating high up in the rafters. I wanted to scream!

Charley said that where we live, bats will only hibernate in attics if the conditions are perfect. And this room didn't look like a random bat hangout. It looked a lot like a little doctor's office, with temperature controls and a table with various instruments and doodads. I found a jar filled with tiny metal tubes. Charley said they were the same type of message tubes used on homing pigeons. Then he started sneezing, so I dragged him downstairs.

Bats + homing-pigeon message tubes = homing bats? Is that what Pop is doing with the bats up there? It would at least explain the stray bats tormenting me at night. *(Shudder again.)* But the big question, of course, is WHY?

Way Later {10:00 pm}

This whole bat thing in the attic is really bothering me. Maybe it's time for another note to my DF.

Dress dummy (of doom).

Sunday, Jan. 1 {10:00am}

The new year is starting off great. Not. Maybe I was a little premature with the whole "life is looking up" thing. Along with bats hiding in my attic and everything else, I had another creepy dream.

I was flying through the night on a white winged horse. The horse was my mother. She was soft and warm, and the night was peaceful. Then out of nowhere, a swarm of bats attacked. But I couldn't scream because I had no mouth. Suddenly my mother vanished in a flash of light. I fell through the dark, clutching her necklace, and woke up to that same Unknown-Noise-Outside-My-Window thing. Totally creepy. Peanut kept watch again.

I couldn't get back to sleep, so I took out the necklace. I've never worn it; it always seemed too special to actually wear, but I put it on then anyway. The stones were warm, like they always were. I felt better and fell asleep.

When I went down for breakfast this morning, Ninny gasped when she saw the necklace. "Your mother's opals!" she cried. "Good Gravy! I forgot all about them! We must wash them dear, or they'll dry out and be useless." She ran the stones under cold water, dried them, and rubbed them with oil. She said the stones need to be cleaned, oiled, and recharged under the full moon once a month. I asked her what they do. She said it's different for everyone who wears them. That doesn't tell me much.

A Little Later {1:00pm}

The last few days I've been collecting information about two rare creatures: the bonnacon and the barometz. They're totally unrelated, but both seem to come from medieval times. I only found a little information on each of them. I'm not sure if I'll get both beasts done today.

Even Later {9:30 pm}

I just found Ninny in front of the parlor windows, waving her hands, burning a smelly twig of something, and muttering with her eyes closed. The floorboards creaked under my feet and startled her. "Oh, Abigail!" she said. "Shhh, dear. Wee Spies are still about. We must protect all entrances to the house." Okay. My necklace is staying on, and Peanut is sleeping on my bed tonight.

Monday, Jan. 2 {8:30 pm}

The first day after vacation is always rough—especially when it's so cold outside that your nose hair freezes on the way to school. To make things worse, Charley's not talking to me.

It started after lunch when Britney strolled over, batting her eyelashes. "Don't forget our lab notes tomorrow, Charley!" His eyes glazed over, and he babbled something nonsensical. She giggled and walked away.

I thought, "Could she be any more obvious?" But I didn't just think it, I said it out loud without realizing. Charley looked confused and asked, "What do you mean?" I blurted out, "You're kidding, right? Charley, why can't you see she's just using you for your brains?"

I immediately wanted to take it back. He got SO mad! He said that maybe everyone wasn't as bad as I judged them to be, that maybe she *liked* him for his brains, and that being his best friend, I could at least support him, especially after everything he was doing for me. He walked away and we haven't spoken since.

I have a huge lump in my stomach. I sent him an email, but he hasn't replied.

Bonnacon

It has horns that curve back so they are useless for fighting; when attacked, it runs away, while releasing a trail of dung that can cover three furlongs. Contact with the dung burns pursuers as though they had touched fire.

PLINY THE ELDER, NATURAL HISTORY, 100 CE

Q. Okay, this is really geeky, but how long is a furlong? A. 1 furlong = 660 feet = 1/8 mile.

Everything I found about the bonnacon was from medieval bestiaries, and they all said the same thing. My guess is that the bonnacon was just a poor bull who ate something that didn't agree with him.

Barometz

It had a head, yes, ears, and all other parts of a newly born lamb.

DESCRIPTION OF THE VEGETABLE LAMB BY SIGISMUND, BARON VON HERBERSTEIN, IN HIS NOTES ON RUSSIA, FROM 1549

Feed me!

A lamb growing out of a plant? Totally weird! This plant grew little fruits that popped open to reveal tiny, perfectly formed lambs, attached to the plant by their belly buttons. The lambs could reach the ground to eat grass, but when the grass was gone, the lambs shriveled up and died—if they didn't get eaten by wolves first.

Help!

SO WHAT'S THE SECRET OF THE BAROMETZ?

Can you stand the suspense? Turn the page and find out. . . .

Charley's still not talking to me. Ugh.

COTTON. Yes, cotton! These strange creatures weren't woolly lambs, they were cottony lambs! Before the 1600s, no one in Europe had ever seen a cotton plant, so when travelers to India, Russia, and China saw these plants with white fuzzy stuff on the buds, they couldn't quite understand how this "wool" grew from a plant. If there was wool, there MUST be a little lamb in there somewhere, right? That's some brilliant logic.

Friday, Jan. 6 {8:00pm}

Of all the times for Charley to be mad at me! I really need his voice of reason right now.

During dinner there was a knock at the front door. Pop answered it, and I peeked into the hall to see who it was. It was Zoey from Bilbo's Books! I heard her say that a few books just came into the store and she thought I might be able to use them for my research. *Uh-oh.* My cover was blown. Pop blocked her from coming in and said, "Thank you very much, but Abigail will NOT be needing those books," before slamming the door in her face. Poor Zoey. What a Pop thing to do. How embarrassing.

Pop marched back to the kitchen, all red-faced. "Did I give you permission to go to the bookstore? I don't appreciate you sneaking around behind my back, young lady."

I hate it when he calls me "young lady." Part of me was afraid he suspected what I was up to, but the other part of me was so mad, I couldn't stop myself from yelling, "Sneaking? What about you, Pop? You're down in the basement all the time doing who knows what—you keep a secret message-delivering bat colony in the attic, and everything is always locked up, including me! You won't even let me get books for homework!" Okay, the homework part was a lie.

He bellowed, "Do not question me. I know what's best for you. You're grounded!"

I yelled back, "How can you ground me when I can't go anywhere anyway!" Then I ran upstairs and locked myself in my room.

So here I sit, friendless and dejected, imprisoned by a tyrannical grandfather in a house full of bats, with a nutty grandmother performing nightly spells to keep an unforeseen danger at bay. I wrote a note to my DF, explaining my plight. Maybe the cat will show up soon.

Saturday, Jan. 7 {11:00am}

Looks like it's going to be a barguest-filled weekend. I'm not leaving my room. I picked up my library books earlier this week, and I have an emergency stash of gingersnaps.

Charley's blocking my instant-message attempts. I sent him twelve more emails. *Please read them, Charley!* If I was a normal teenager, I'd have a cell phone and I could bombard him with text messages.

Sunday, Jan. 8 {7:30pm}

Ninny thinks I'm sick, so she's been bringing me chicken soup and peanut butter sandwiches all weekend. Note to self: do not feed peanut butter to Peanut. It smells like a bonnacon habitat in here.

Sweet peanut butter,
Stuck to the roof of my mouth.
Salty, gloppy goo.

HAIKU

All down the church in midst of fire, the hellish monster flew.

And, passing onward to the quire, he many people slew.

PART OF AN OLD POEM, DESCRIBING THE BLACK DOG OF BUNGAY

This weather vane is on the town square in Bungay, England. On the morning of August 4, 1577 CE, during a violent storm, a giant black dog burst into a church in the middle of Sunday mass. Legend says it killed several people in a riot of fire and fury. Naturally, they all thought it was the devil.

For hundreds of years, people from all over Europe, especially the British Isles, say they've seen the phantom black dog. Most of the time it appears as a big, black, shaggy dog with glowing red eyes. But is it a real animal, or a ghost?

Common Characteristics

It appears out of nowhere and then vanishes.
It lives near cemeteries and at road crossings.
It's an omen of death—people die after they see it.
But sometimes it follows people to protect them.

I have to admit, Peanut looks a bit like a barquest. Hmmm....

Bogey Beast

Padfoot

103

Tuesday, Jan. 10 {6:00pm}

Today was so eventful that I need to divide the happenings into two parts.

Part 1: I got sent to the principal's office. First time ever in my life. Ugh. I wonder what Pop will have to say about this. But good news—Charley's talking to me again!

In the hallway today, at the peak of the after-school locker rush, Charley walked up to the Britneys with a flower in his hand. He had mentioned the Winter Festival dance last week, so my guess was that he planned to ask Britney #1. I sensed impending doom. She cackled. Her voice carried over the crowd. "Oh, pumpkin. I wouldn't be caught dead at a dance with you!" Poor Charley. He deflated within an instant.

Everyone laughed. I couldn't take it. I couldn't just stand there and let Charley be ridiculed. I walked over, fully intending to yell at her, but all I heard from my mouth was a squeak. She looked me up and down and said, "Oh, wait, Abigail wants to say something! Haven't you said enough in your journal, Miss Beast Hunter?" More laughter. Then I don't know what came over me. I felt a surge of energy and I punched her. Right in the mouth. The hallway fell silent.

Lucky me. Mr. Sykes, the principal, was walking by. He asked someone to take Britney to the nurse and offered to escort me to his office.

At least he wasn't mean. Like I said, I've never been to the principal's office. He did the "I'm disappointed in you, Abigail" thing and then "Is everything okay at home?" He said he would have to call my grandfather.

Charley said he's going to start calling me "slugger." I now await the phone call of doom.

POW

Part 2: After the punching nonsense, as Charley and I were walking home, I remembered I had a note for the cat. It did finally show its furry face. But it didn't come up to me like it usually does. It ran away. Charley and I ran after it, down by the lake, along a deserted dirt road, up to a cottage with a serious Hansel and Gretel vibe.

The cat meowed at the front door. Guess who opened it? Miss Malkin! She said with an evil grin, "Good afternoon, children. Abigail, I daresay your grandfather won't be pleased with you being here." We must have looked terrified because she laughed and said, "Don't worry, I'm not going to throw you into the oven." I wasn't so sure. . . .

I blurted out, "You . . . the notes . . . the cat." She chuckled, "Oh, I just provide the delivery service, dear." Charley fired off questions at her, but she chuckled again. She said we should try asking my grandfather for answers first. If he won't reveal what he's hiding, she said we should come back and see her. Then I remembered the note in my pocket. As I pulled it out, she said, "Yes, I'll deliver that for you," took the note, and shut the door.

We ran home as fast as we could without freezing our lungs. I can't believe Pop is somehow connected to this. The thought of confronting him is overwhelming.

Later {9:30 pm}

The phone call of doom arrived. Pop said I was "extremely irresponsible." I can't leave my room now, except to go to school. Peanut, centaurs, and homework are keeping me company. At least I'm not friendless anymore.

Hello? Hello? It's DOOM calling!

105

Wednesday, Jan. 11 {4:30 pm}

In anticipation of the consequences of yesterday's incident, my left armpit started sweating on the walk to school. Charley stayed home sick today—that run home from Miss Malkin's proved to be too much for him. I'd be facing the music alone. Britney and Kane would have the whole eighth grade turned against me by lunch.

And so my day began with this note in my locker. Totally unexpected.

Then Deke stopped me in the hall and said, "Yo, Ab. Quite the buzz this morning." I so eloquently replied, "Uh, yeah." He nodded his head, said, "Sweet. Abigail acts on behalf of the downtrodden," then walked away.

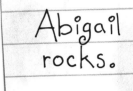

Abigail rocks.

My day continued in this unexpected direction, with kids smiling at me left and right. It was really weird. It felt kind of good, but I also had this weird guilty feeling.

I didn't see Britney #1 until third-period English. She sneered at me with her swollen lip. The other Britneys surrounded her in a protective circle. "She thinks she's so *tough*. Don't worry, she'll get hers," they said. Then Kane and his minions walked in with a whole battery of "slugger" comments. Even though Britney #1 was such a jerk, I almost wanted to apologize. Almost.

The biggest weirdness came at lunch. The Band and Art Geeks invited me to sit at their table. Naturally, my powers of speech vanished. Everyone gave me props and pats on the back, then the talk turned to new movies, music, gossip—stuff that I am clueless about. I'm sure it didn't take long for them to realize why I was never invited to sit at their table before. I was a fish out of water. As soon as I finished eating, I got up, kind of waved at everyone, then escaped to my hiding spot in the library.

Later {8:00 pm}

I'm sitting here trying to solve algebra equations, but I can't stop thinking about these two things. I keep telling myself it's just my imagination, but things are adding up.

Thing 1: I've been wearing my mother's necklace ever since that bad dream I had a while back. Since then, I've noticed that whenever I get angry or afraid, the necklace starts to buzz. I swear. Then the buzzing goes into my chest and kind of energizes me. It's happened twice. First, the night Zoey came to the door, when I yelled at Pop—I've never been able to talk back to him like that. Then yesterday, when I slugged Britney—I don't quite know where that came from. Maybe Ninny was right about the stones having powers. Part of that poem from her journal said: "O mighty stone of fiery black, strengthen the body to stand attack." Could it be true?

Thing 2: Peanut. I can't get the whole barguest thing out of my head. Looking back over the years, there are so many things I never noticed. Like the fact that he *never* leaves our yard. He's stuck to me like glue in the house, you'd think he would have tried to follow me at some point, right? And he's really old for a dog—at least as old as I am—and he shows no signs of aging. And if I'd been paying attention to his whining, I'd have realized that he always knows when something is about to happen—like when bats fly down on my head. I know most dogs follow their people, but maybe there's more to Peanut. What if he really is a barguest?

Charley's going over to Bilbo's Books for me to see if he can find anything on centaurs and Bigfoot. Wow, only two more beasts on my list. I'm almost done and still nothing terrible has happened.

necklace?

Magical dog?

Centaurs were dignified, noble, and wise creatures...

...for the most part. They had one teeny flaw. Sometimes they did crazy stuff like start fights and carry off young maidens. That gave them a bit of an image problem. I can relate.

Family
Dad: King Ixion
Mom: a cloud; centaurs must all be brothers.

Home
Mount Pelion, Greece

Diet
Raw meat

Skills
Archery
Philosophy

THE CENTAUR OF VOLOS

This is the closest I've come to concrete physical evidence. A real skeleton with all its parts would prove that centaurs really existed, right? But no. It's fake. *(Sighs with disappointment.)* It's an exhibit called "Centaur Excavations at Volos" at the John C. Hodges Library at the University of Tennessee. Its intention is to force people to examine the facts.

My incredibly BRILLIANT {but not very scientific} IDEAS

CENTAURS COULD IN FACT BE:

Men on Horseback

This seems like it might be a plausible theory. Back in ancient Greece, there were no horses. But in the lands to the north, there were cattle-herding dudes who rode horses, just like the cowboys in the Old West. So, at some point in time, cowboys from the north met up with the Greeks in the south, who mistook the horse and rider for a creepy horse/man monstrosity.

The same thing happened to the native people in South America when they first met Spanish soldiers on horseback. They were terrified! (Of course it didn't help that the soldiers were attacking them at the time.)

What kind of monster is that?

Thursday, Jan. 12 {6:30am}

There was one more Unknown-Noise-Outside-My-Window Incident last night. Peanut was already whining and pacing at the window when I woke up. The noise woke Ninny up, too. She came in and waved her hands around the windows, mumbling about danger and spies.

Later {4:00pm}

More weirdness today! When I got home from school, Ninny was waiting for me at the door with a box in her arms. She said, "I remembered! Abigail, I remembered the secret! Up to your room—quickly!"

We rushed upstairs. Ninny propped a chair in front of the door, pulled down the window shade, checked under the bed for Wee Spies and handed me the box. She didn't remember what was in the box, only that it was very important. It was really fancy—covered in leather, with brass corners. On the lid was a big medallion, inscribed with the words "Mystic Phyles."

But then we heard Pop climbing the stairs—making sure I was home from school, no doubt. Ninny said, "Quick, hide the box. Your grandfather won't like this. Guard it with your life!" She hurried out of my room to divert Pop.

I waited until I knew Ninny and Pop were downstairs, and then I opened the box. It was filled with old folders. Each folder contained a collection of information about a different beast—the same beasts I've been researching! I can't tell what it all means. Now along with doing Bigfoot research, I need to look at these files.

Bigfoot

Mongolian name: Almas

Australian name: Yowie

Himalayan name: Yeti

Canadian name: Sasquatch

These big hairy guys have been spotted on every continent in the world except Antarctica, right up to the present day.

In 1958, in the Northern California woods, a construction worker named Jerry Crew found huge footprints. He made a plaster cast of one of the prints and took it to the local newspaper. They published a story about it, calling the creature "Bigfoot."

COMMON BEHAVIORS

Nocturnal
Most often they're seen or heard at night.

Solitary
They live alone or in small family groups.

Curious
When spotted, they often watch people, then calmly walk away.

Mischievous
They haven't been known to attack people, but they'll steal food and mess up campsites.

This photograph shows Loren Coleman, one of the best-known cryptozoologists in the world, holding a replica of the original Jerry Crew footprint cast.

THE EVIDENCE

Scientists still can't say Bigfoot is real. One big reason is that they don't have a body. But there are other types of evidence.

Feces is poop!

Sighting Reports

Thousands of people around the world have seen large, hairy, manlike creatures in remote woods.

Hair, Blood, Skin & Feces

Bits of this gross stuff have been collected from nests and examined by scientists who say that the samples don't match any known animals. Hello! Doesn't that prove *something*?

Photos & Video

People have taken lots of photos and home movies of Bigfoot. Unfortunately none of them are very good.

Charley and I borrowed a gorilla suit from the drama department and tried to recreate the most famous Bigfoot video of all time—in his backyard. The original film, called the Patterson-Gimlin film (named after its creators), was shot in California in 1967. It's been picked apart by hundreds, if not thousands, of scientists and researchers, and no one has been able to prove for certain if it's real or a hoax.

That gorilla suit was itchy!

Footprints

Next to sightings, footprints make up the biggest chunk of evidence. Some plaster casts of footprints are so detailed that they show cracks and ridges in the skin. Some prints are as long as 17 inches!

The relative size of my foot to a Bigfoot foot. Now that's a big foot!

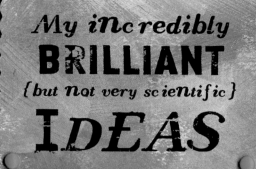

My incredibly BRILLIANT
{but not very scientific}
IDEAS

BIGFOOT COULD IN FACT BE:

1

A Mysterious Species of Hominin

The term *hominin* describes modern humans and our evolutionary ancestors. The Neanderthal man, one of those ancestors, became extinct about 30,000 years ago. But what if they or another unknown hominin survived in remote areas of the world? I found some interesting research by a man named Bill Munns, an expert in movie makeup effects. He has spent a great deal of time analyzing the Patterson-Gimlin footage to determine if the creature was a man in a suit. He found remarkable similarities between the proportions of the creature and those of the Neanderthal.

FIGURE 1

Outline of the proportions of the creature in the Patterson-Gimlin film, with a skeleton superimposed.

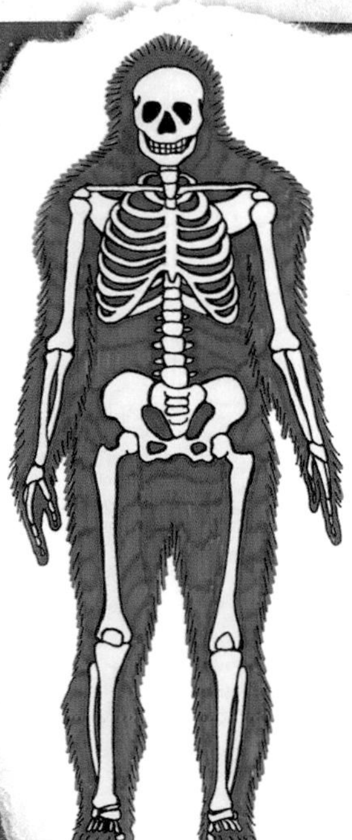

FIGURE 2

Half of the Bigfoot skeleton from figure 1 on the left side, compared to half of a Neanderthal skeleton on the right side.

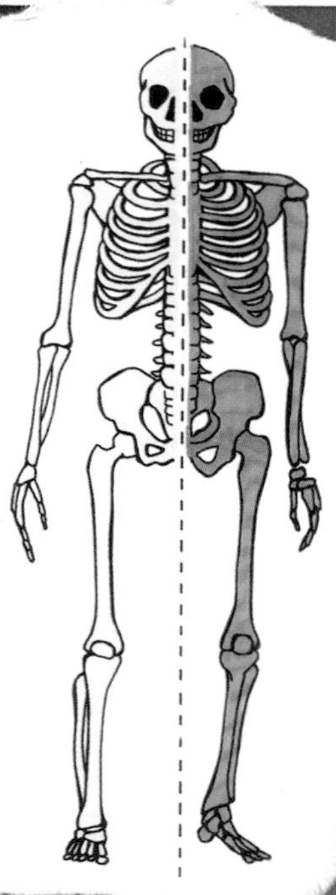

The two skeleton halves look so much alike!

116

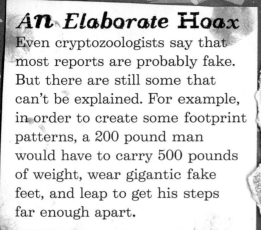

2 An Elaborate Hoax

Even cryptozoologists say that most reports are probably fake. But there are still some that can't be explained. For example, in order to create some footprint patterns, a 200 pound man would have to carry 500 pounds of weight, wear gigantic fake feet, and leap to get his steps far enough apart.

3 A Worldwide Hallucination

Around the world, there have been more sightings of Bigfoot than any other creature. That's pretty incredible. Can ALL of those people be wrong?

I'm not sure if I believe this, but Bigfoot could be some sort of group hallucination. Here's how it might work: One person sees what they think is Bigfoot and runs home to tell the story. The story spreads. Then other people claim to see it, either because they're dying to see it, too, or they're afraid of it, or it's the first thing that pops into their heads when they spy something strange. Could this really happen on a worldwide scale?

Friday, Jan. 13 {6:30am}

After finishing my Bigfoot pages last night, I stayed up late to read through the Mystic Phyles. And I found something to convince me that all of these beasts are REAL. The folders are grouped by species. Within each folder, individual creatures have their own classification records, listing things like breed, portal of origin (what's that?), containment location (huh?), along with notes about preferred climate, intelligence, etc. Well, in the barguest folder, guess what I found? A record for Peanut! Peanut is his code name, and his "containment location" is HERE! The implications of this are huge.

First, the information in these files is ten times more overwhelming than my own research. It's basically the same stuff, just way more extensive—and professional. From what I've seen so far, there are sighting logs and reports, beast classification charts, newspaper clippings, drawings, and more—hundreds of years' worth of gathering—all recorded by people called "Keepers" with no names, only identification numbers.

Does this mean that Ninny and Pop are involved with these Keepers? Are THEY Keepers? Why else would Ninny have the Phyles? Why else would Peanut be here? What's the purpose of all this information?

Everything has to be related—the notes in Ninny's travel journals, Pop's bat colony in the attic, the Mystic Phyles, Peanut's secret identity, the Keepers, the warning letter from the Board of Mystical Management, my Devoted Friend, Miss Malkin—but how is it all connected?

Is Peanut a fugitive beast in a relocation program?

Later {4:30 pm}

Help! Charley and I locked ourselves in my room. We don't know what to do. After school, we decided to search The Room for anything related to the Mystic Phyles or Keepers. Pop was in the basement, and Ninny was cooking dinner, so we figured the coast was clear.

We found something, all right. But it wasn't what we were looking for. We found something really creepy—boxes of blank BoMM stationery! The same stationery used to write the letter they mailed to me!

And just then—the timing couldn't have been more perfect—POP CAME UP THE STAIRS. There wasn't time for us to hide. Pop said my name in a very "what are you doing up here" kind of voice. When he walked in and saw the stationery in our hands, he looked shocked. He came toward me, and my instinct told me to run. Charley and I bolted to my room with Peanut on our heels, just in time to lock ourselves in. Pop called after me, "Abigail, you need to understand. It was only to protect you!" He pounded on my door, telling me I couldn't stay in my room forever. He *thinks* I can't stay in here forever. *Just watch me!*

This is just too scary. Pop just admitted he sent me that letter! I can't think of any good reason for my own grandfather to scare me like that. Miss Malkin was right. He's hiding something and I don't know whom to trust. Does Ninny belong to the BoMM, too? How does this relate to the Mystic Phyles and the Keepers?

So Charley and I are locked in my room with Peanut and the Mystic Phyles. My necklace is buzzing. I wish it came with a user manual.

Signing off now. Hopefully not for the last time.

BoMM

DOOM AWAITS!

HELP!!

119

Saturday, Jan. 14 {9:00am}

Every time I think things can't get any worse, guess what happens? They get worse! Last night, Charley and I were still locked in my room, reading through folders in the Mystic Phyles. Around midnight, Peanut started growling and pacing around. Then there was a huge crash downstairs. Ninny yelled for my help, so we ran out and she dragged us downstairs.

At the bottom of the stairs, we were hit with a blast of cold air from the kitchen. I could see that the wall of windows at the back of the kitchen had been completely smashed. Snow and wind swirled in. Then I heard it. The Unknown-Noise-Outside-My-Window! And there was Pop, waving a sword in the air. As soon as we ran into the kitchen, huge shadows swooped down on us: giant batlike monsters—three of them—with four-foot wingspans and bodies like monkeys. Just like ahools!

It was total confusion. My feet were frozen in place. Snow and wind; glass everywhere; dishes, cans, and jars crashed to the floor, swept off the shelves by the beating wings of the bats.

Then a bat dove straight for my head. Pop jumped in front of me, threatening the bat with his sword. Shrieking and swerving, the bat's claws grazed the side of my face.

Pop turned to see if I was all right, but a split second later he was knocked to the ground. The bat clutched Pop's chest, then plunged its fangs into his shoulder. Pop called to me through clenched teeth, "Run! Abigail, Charley, run!" The sword slid from his hand, and he went limp.

Peanut's eyes turned a glowing red. From his mouth came an unearthly, earsplitting sound. The bats all dropped to the ground, squealing and writhing. Charley yelled over the noise, "He's disabling their echolocation!" I remembered this from my ahool research. Bats basically *see* with their ears. Peanut was jamming their signals!

Then the same bat that took Pop down hooked its finger claw around Charley's ankle and sank its teeth into his calf. Charley fell to his knees. "Venomous . . . bat . . . ," he said, his voice trailing off. And he passed out.

"NO!" My necklace was buzzing like crazy. I frantically located Pop's sword, heaved it up, and drove it through the bat. The bat screamed and twitched. Blood bubbled from its wound, and a tremor of disgust shook my arms and legs. I dragged Pop and Charley away from the other two writhing monstrosities, which were now agitated by the smell of fresh blood spreading across the floor. Pop and Charley were turning greenish. Not good.

I knew I needed to stop the other two, and fast. I had no idea how much longer Peanut could continue the deafening sound. Trying to keep my stomach from lurching up into my throat, I braced myself to stab Bat #2, just as Charley's grandparents burst out of the basement. *The basement?*

Charley's grandfather yelled, "Don't kill them! They need to be preserved! They're highly intelligent! Abigail, go find some blankets!"

Charley's grandmother called to Ninny, "Veneno vampire bats! Aurelia, we don't have much time!" She pulled tiny packets of powders and herbs out of her giant feathered bag. As I ran to the hall closet for blankets, the two old ladies started mixing potions to bring Pop and Charley back from the edge of green death.

121

When I got back to the kitchen, Mr. Winkley threw the blankets down on top of the bats and showed me what to do. The smell of blood and the sight of those wriggling bodies made me want to throw up, but I forced myself to help him wrap and tie the bats in the blankets. My fingers were freezing up from the cold air coming through the broken windows, and my head was pounding from Peanut's deafening noise, but within several minutes, we immobilized the bats, and Peanut fell into an exhausted heap.

Ninny and Mrs. Winkley hurried to cover Pop's and Charley's wounds with smelly herbal gunk and bandages. We carried them upstairs, out of the cold, and tucked them in bed—Pop in his bed and Charley in mine. Mrs. Winkley said that Veneno vampire venom can be lethal, but the combination of cold air (which slowed down Pop's and Charley's circulation) and the herbal gunk will hopefully prevent any lasting damage. She thinks they'll be okay, but we won't know for sure until they wake up.

As soon as Pop and Charley were settled, Mr. Winkley turned to Ninny with a grave look. "Aurelia, we have a problem. The files . . . they're gone." He told her that as soon as our house came under attack, Pop called him. He and Mrs. Winkley rushed down to the chamber where the files were hidden, but they were too late. (Apparently, our houses are connected by an underground tunnel. How cool is that?) Someone had already breached the basement security and stolen the files.

"Are these files, by any chance, called, Mystic Phyles?" I asked. They all turned to me, eyes wide. I took that as a yes and reminded Ninny that she gave them to me for safekeeping. Obviously, she forgot.

Mr. Winkley dropped to his knees and yelled, "Hallelujah!" He said he hadn't been so happy since the Red Sox won the World Series.

At least one thing is clear: the bat attack was a diversion. Somebody *really* wants the Mystic Phyles. But who? And why? I pleaded with them to tell me.

They all just looked at each other. Mrs. Winkley said she wished they could tell me, but it was up to Pop. In the meantime, she said they needed to secure the files as quickly as possible. Since the intruders didn't find what they wanted, they might still be lurking about. I didn't relish the idea of another attack, especially in my room, where the files were hidden, so I figured it was probably best to hand them over. I went to my room (Charley was still unconscious), got them, and gave Mr. Winkley the box. He disappeared downstairs.

At that point, Ninny alerted me to the fact that I was a mess—the gashes on my cheek were burning, and cuts and scratches covered my hands. She cleaned me up and I'm now back in my room. I'm very tired, but I can't fall asleep. I need to watch over Charley. And Peanut. Poor Peanut. He dragged himself upstairs and collapsed on the floor. I gave him the biggest hug ever and scratched behind his ears. He licked my nose once, flopped his head down, and started snoring.

Later {2:15pm}

I must have fallen asleep on top of Peanut because when I woke up, I was spitting out dog fur and Charley was mumbling. He said something about bats, but then he passed out. I went to find the Winkleys to alert them. They were just coming out of Ninny and Pop's room.

Pop was awake. He looked terrible—shrunken and weak—not the Pop I'm used to. When he realized I was in the room, he rasped, "Abigail, you could have been killed. The letter—I sent the letter so you would stop the research—to keep you safe."

I asked why. He said he needed to uphold the laws, and that I was safer if I knew nothing. I tried to ask him more, but, even whispering, he was still Pop. He said, "I will tell you no more." I left in defeat.

Before I walked in there, I felt terrible that he almost died. Now I want to scream at him. My necklace is buzzing like mad. I feel strong enough to throw the bed across the room, but I'm helpless against Pop.

A Little Later {3:00pm}

Ninny took me downstairs for a snack. The kitchen was still cold, but most of the mess was gone. Mr. Winkley took the bats away (who knows where to). He also nailed boards over the broken windows and cleaned up all the glass and blood.

I wasn't really hungry, but Ninny took out some cookies and made hot chocolate. While I nibbled at my cookie, Ninny blew on my hot chocolate like she did when I was little. I really wish Ninny wasn't so nuts. If she could remember, I bet she would tell me what's going on. She wouldn't keep me in the dark.

She put her arm around me and patted my necklace. She said it was protecting me well.

Even Later {9:15pm}

After my snack, I nodded off at my desk. I woke up to mumbling noises from Charley. It took him a few minutes to come around. But as soon as his eyes were fully open, he started marveling at how a bat with such potent venom must be extremely rare and how we must look to see if it's listed in the Mystic Phyles.

I'm so relieved that he's okay. I filled him in on the rest of the day's events and told him that his grandfather now possessed the Phyles—I had no way of looking up the Veneno vampire bat.

Since they don't want to move Charley yet, Ninny's making up a spare bedroom for me. Peanut, my trusty Barguest, will be sleeping by my side. I love that I have my very own mythical beast.

Sunday, Jan. 15 {8:30am}

I didn't sleep well in the spare room. Weird dreams. I came in early to check on Charley. He was awake, so we started talking, trying to make sense of the pieces we had so far.

First off, we determined that Ninny, Pop, and Charley's grandparents are obviously working together. Since they're protecting the Mystic Phyles, and have Peanut here, they *must* be Keepers. So maybe Pop's BoMM letter really was just a decoy, like he said.

Second, when my DF said that there are those who would hide the truth, he must have been referring to Pop. And he told me not to exercise heroic efforts. Does that mean that he knew about the bat attack beforehand and didn't want me to get hurt? At any rate it seems pretty clear that my DF and Miss Malkin are *not* on Pop's side.

But we still don't know why the Phyles are so important—or why I'm in the middle.

We decided to ask Charley's grandmother again. We begged her to tell us how it was all connected as she made Charley some horrible medicine.

She gave a discouraged sigh that ruffled the feathers on her hat. She said she agreed that we should know the truth. But she was loyal to Pop, even if she didn't agree with him. I asked her if there was any way at all to convince him to tell us the truth. She said there might be a way. But I had to be willing to stand up to Pop. If I could do it, she and Mr. Winkley would back me up. If it's the only way to get to the bottom of everything, I'll do it.

Later {4:00 pm}

Pop slept all morning, so Ninny gave us the green light when he woke up. We all marched into his room—Charley's grandparents, a wobbly but determined Charley, and me.

Pop looked suspicious. With my feet firmly planted on the floor by his bed, I took a deep breath and said, "Pop, you need to tell me what's going on here. It's not fair to keep it from me any longer."

"We've already discussed this," he said.

I told him that since this could now be a matter of life and death, I deserved to know. He said that was precisely why I *shouldn't* know, and folded his arms across his chest.

It was time to pull out my weapon. I replied, "Miss Malkin said you wouldn't tell me anything. And the notes I've been getting from my Devoted Friend say I shouldn't trust people who are hiding the truth! Since you're not going to tell me, I'm going back to her. She'll tell me."

Fury rose on Pop's face and he said, "You will do no such thing! All these years I've kept you safe, protected you, and this is how you thank me? After all I've sacrificed for you! What has Miss Malkin ever done for you? She's wrong if she thinks she can plant the seeds of mistrust in you and destroy my life's work."

Charley's grandmother spoke up. "Alistair, if you insist on keeping the truth from Abigail, you're going to lose her! Look at what's happening! Don't let history repeat itself. She's old enough to think for herself. She already knows about the Mystic Phyles. She's figured out that we're all Keepers. Keeping the rest from her now will only push her away. You need her loyalty, Alistair."

Pop closed his eyes and sat like a stone. I figured that was it. His mind was made up and it was no use. I started out the door. I said I was leaving and going to find Miss Malkin. He yelled, "No! Abigail, come back here! You will not leave this house!" I started slowly down the stairs. And then, in a softer voice came, "Abigail, come back. Please. I will tell you."

My threat had worked.

The Download

Pop began with the obvious, the Keepers. He said I was right in assuming that he and Ninny and the Winkleys were all Keepers. He said Charley's parents are Keepers, too, as were my parents—and that Charley and I would also become Keepers. I guess it's like the family business. But there are also thousands of other Keepers around the world.

Since the beginning of recorded time, the Keepers have been studying fantastical beings. And there are many more classifications besides the beasts. Some are dangerous and powerful, some are harmless and meek, and some even look human. The Keepers protect them all.

I couldn't understand why they all needed to be hidden away. But then Pop asked me to imagine what would happen if they were found. At first I thought it would be magnificent. How awesome would it be to live in a world with magical creatures roaming around? But then I realized that in this world, there was no way they could roam freely. First of all, some of them, like dragons, could be downright dangerous. They'd be locked up in zoos or laboratories, or killed for their skins, horns, magical feathers, etc. Or they'd be used as weapons, like the Veneno vampire bats.

Then Pop shared the big reason why Mr. and Mrs. Winkley wouldn't tell me anything. They were being loyal to Pop because . . . he's the boss. The big boss. His title is Grand Keeper. He's in charge of ALL the Keepers. Everywhere. And that's not all. There's more. When he retires, I'm supposed to take his place. *(Jaw drops to floor.)*

Pop said my Devoted Friend wanted to plant seeds of mistrust between Pop and me. I'm important to Pop's enemies because I'm their chance to take control of everything the Keepers protect. Swaying Keepers to their side has been one of their greatest weapons. And now they're trying to sway me, the Grand Keeper's heir. It's a great plan, and Miss Malkin is in on it. When it's my time to become Grand Keeper, they're hoping I'll turn against Pop and expose what the Keepers have safely hidden for thousands of years.

Abigail Thaddeus: high-powered leader of a secret organization or plain old dorky teenager?

Then Pop got very serious. He said he's taken a great chance in trusting me and Charley, and we must swear our loyalty to the Keepers. Usually there's a whole big official ceremony when a Keeper is inducted at the age of eighteen. But given the unusual circumstances, we had to swear on Ninny and Pop's bed linens to guard the secrets of the Mystic Phyles.

Oh yeah, and the bats in the attic? They're exactly what Charley guessed. A nearly undetectable, secret message-delivering army.

Even Later {9:00 pm}

At least I know the truth now. Everything makes sense—Pop keeping me cloistered here, his basement dungeon, the locked rooms upstairs, the stories in Ninny's journals, the message-delivering bats swooping around—it's all because Pop is the leader of a supersecret organization.

And I'm going to take over when he retires, which, since he's so old, might be soon. But I have no experience with anything. How am I supposed to run a worldwide secret organization? I can barely manage algebra! This makes me wish even more that my parents were still alive. How did they deal with knowing that the fate of the world would someday rest in their hands?

On the flip side, I wonder if this means I'll get to travel. Maybe Charley and I will get to meet other kids like us. He'd better keep himself from getting sick. I don't want to go anywhere without him.

Monday, Jan. 16 {4:30pm}

Charley has to stay home another day, so I went to school today alone. I still had Band-Aids on my hands and the lovely gashes on my cheek, but I went about my day pretty much unnoticed. Deke asked me if I got into another tangle with the Britneys. I was happy to answer no to that one. And Kane left me alone, which was a nice stroke of luck. Until after school.

After making up an algebra test, I arrived at my locker later than usual, and the hall was empty. As I packed up my bag, Kane turned the corner. Alone. My stroke of luck was definitely over.

He walked up to my locker, and I put my hand to my mother's necklace as I stared him down. But then Kane said, "Um, whatever happened," pointing at the Band-Aids on my hands, "I hope you're okay." He looked uncomfortable and fidgety, and of all things, SINCERE! And I can't even believe I'm going to say this. Okay, here goes. For an itsy-bitsy, teeny-weeny second, he actually looked CUTE.

But then his minions rounded the corner. Sincere was replaced by sinister, and they all danced away in a cloud of jeers and laughter. He is still SO my archenemy.

Pop is up on his feet today and back to his old self. As soon as I got home, he said, "I hope you realize that you are still expected home from school right away, young lady." *Sigh.* So much for my fantasy of getting to travel and meet other Keepers.

Incidentally, Ninny is celebrating "Nothing Day" today. She's sitting in the kitchen, doing nothing—not even talking. I wonder what this means for dinner tonight.

Tuesday, Jan. 17 {3:45pm}

The cat appeared this morning with another note. My DF obviously knows about the bat attack. I guess this confirms Pop's theory. Pop said that he wants me to keep communicating with my DF—he wants to use the DF's trust in me to lure him out. This, of course, means that I have to show all my DF notes to Pop.

I do believe in the Keepers. I really do. But there's something about the notes—I can't help feeling intrigued. There *is* that pesky little detail of not knowing who my DF is, though. Maybe I'm just being manipulated. Pop's probably right.

ANOTHER NOTE!

Dearest Abigail,

News of the recent events
in Westbrook has reached me.
I am thankful you are alive.

You are to be congratulated on your
research progress. Soon you will realize the great value of this knowledge.

You must continue! Charley may help you
now. Remember, you are more important
than you know. Stay safe.

Your next topic—faeries—awaits!

Your Devoted Friend

I haven't shown the note to Pop yet. I know. I should. Why am I making this complicated? Obviously Pop is the good guy and this DF person is the bad guy. I know the Keepers are right. But I can't help but wonder if Pop's main concern is his duty as Grand Keeper. He's so obsessed with keeping me safe. But is that for my own sake, or the sake of the Keepers? Maybe if my parents were alive, and Pop didn't have to worry so much about who was going to take over, he'd be retired by now and could have been more grandfatherly—like Charley's grandfather. I guess running a worldwide supersecret organization while keeping track of a grandkid and a nutty wife must be stressful.

Later {7:30 pm}

Okay, I did the right thing and showed the note to Pop. He didn't say anything after he read it. He just nodded and gave the note back to me with a look on his face that was so extremely sad. It was startling. I've never seen him look like that before.

On the bright side, I'm excited about starting my next research project. Faeries await. Charley's totally into it. He's making lists of books for us to order from the library. Well, my journal is out of pages, so it's time to sign off. And I have to study for end-of-semester tests. Ugh. I need a snack. Maybe I'll try an apple—Charley keeps pestering me about the healthy snacking thing.

Abigail Thaddeus

Sprays juice everywhere,
When I bite into its skin.
Red shiny apple.

HAIKU

WOW, I'm done! And I survived. DOUBLE WOW.

Now that I know mythical beasts are real, I have a whole new perspective on faeries. Here's what I want to find out:

- Is there more to the faerie realm than stereotypical little creatures with wings?
- How many different kinds of faerie creatures are there?
- Do they live here on earth or in another world that somehow intersects with ours?
- Are faeries friendly? Or should I be afraid of them?

(Cue music of doom here.)
♪ ♪ ♫ ♩ ♩

Hey, where'd this come from?

These are the books I used:

Although I used lots of books, these were the most useful. A few of them are old and hard to find, but librarians (even creepy ones like Miss Malkin) are always good about helping you find any kind of book.

Barber, Richard, and Anne Riches. *A Dictionary of Fabulous Beasts*. New York: Walker and Company, 1971.

Benwell, Gwen, and Arthur Waugh. *Sea Enchantress*. New York: Citadel Press, 1965.

Coleman, Loren, and Jerome Clark. *Cryptozoology A to Z*. New York: Fireside, 1999.

Coleman, Loren, and Patrick Huyghe. *The Field Guide to Bigfoot, Yeti, and Other Mystery Primates Worldwide*. New York: Avon Books, Inc., 1999.

Ellis, Richard. *Monsters of the Sea*. New York: Alfred A. Knopf, 1994.

Heuvelmans, Bernard. *In the Wake of the Sea-Serpents*. New York: Hill and Wang, 1969.

Ley, Willy. *Willy Ley's Exotic Zoology*. New York: Viking Press, 1959.

Nigg, Joseph. *The Book of Dragons & Other Mythical Beasts*. New York: Barron's Educational Series, Inc., 2002.

Nigg, Joseph. *Fabulous Beasts*. New York: Oxford University Press, 1999.

Nigg, Joseph. *Wonder Beasts*. Englewood, CO: Libraries Unlimited, Inc., 1995.

Rose, Carol. *Giants, Monsters & Dragons*. New York: W. W. Norton & Company, 2000.

Trubshaw, Bob. *Explore Phantom Black Dogs*. Loughborough, UK: Heart of Albion Press, Explore Books, 2005.

Zell-Ravenheart, Oberon, and Ash "LeopardDancer" DeKirk. *A Wizard's Bestiary*. Franklin Lakes, NJ: The Career Press, Inc., New Page Books, 2007.

In case I really do whatever and my journal is launched to fame, I want to make sure everybody knows where to find their own information.

These are the pictures I used:

I don't want to break any copyright laws (all I need is to become a criminal at the age of 13), so I've tried to list all the sources for photographs and illustrations that I didn't create myself.

Page 11. House photographs courtesy of Benjamin Faucher.

Page 13. Mermaid courtesy of Dover Publications.

Page 15. Feejee mermaid courtesy of Loren Coleman.

Page 17. Oannes from Sabine Baring-Gould, *Curious Myths of the Middle Ages* (London, Oxford and Cambridge: Rivingtons, 1873), page 495.

Page 23. Mermaid monster courtesy of the U.S. National Library of Medicine.

Page 29. Sea monster courtesy of the U.S. National Library of Medicine.

Page 30 (top). Olaus Magnus Carta Marina courtesy of the James Ford Bell Library, University of Minnesota, Minneapolis, Minnesota.

Page 30 (bottom). Cape Ann serpent reprinted by permission of the MIT Museum.

Page 34. Whale skin from J. Murray and J. Hjort, *The Depths of the Ocean: A General Account of the Modern Science of Oceanography Based Largely on the Scientific Researches of the Norwegian Steamer 'Michael Sars' in the North Atlantic* (London: Macmillan and Co., Ltd., 1912).

Page 35 (top). Guam shipwreck courtesy of Joe and Cyndy Pruski.

Page 35 (middle). Lock Ness photograph courtesy of Stephanie Brockway and Ralph Masiello.

Page 41. House fire courtesy of the West Brookfield Fire Department, anonymous contributor.

Page 57. Challicum bunyip reproduced from *The Victorian Naturalist* with permission from the editors.

Page 61. Pterodactyls from "Note on the Pterodactyle Tribe Considered as Marsupial Bats." *The Zoologist,* 1843, Volume 1, page 129.

Page 79. Eclipse reprinted with permission of Steve Albers, Dennis diCicco, and Gary Emerson.

Page 83 (middle). Bellerophon mosaic medallion courtesy of Musée Rolin, Autun, France, a location of the National Archaeological Museum of Saint-Germain-en-Laye. Photograph by P. Veysseyre.

Page 83 (bottom). Origami Pegasus directions and design by Anibal Voyer.

Page 88. Unicorn courtesy of the U.S. National Library of Medicine.

Page 91. "Bull With Single Horn Is Modern Unicorn." *Popular Science,* July 1936, page 14.

Page 97. Bonnacon from the *Aberdeen Bestiary,* AU MS 24. Reproduced with permission from the University of Aberdeen, United Kingdom.

Page 99. Vegetable lamb from H. Lee, *The Vegetable Lamb of Tartary: A Curious Fable of the Cotton Plant, to Which Is Added a Sketch of the History of Cotton and the Cotton Trade* (London: S. Low, Marston, Searle & Rivington, 1887).

Page 103. Peanut courtesy of Frank and Patty White.

Page 109 (top). Centaur courtesy of Pearson Scott Foresman.

Page 109 (bottom). Centaur skeleton constructed by William Withers. "Centaur Excavations at Volos" exhibit created by Beauvais Lyons at the John C. Hodges Library, University of Tennessee. Photograph courtesy of the University of Tennessee Libraries.

Page 113. Loren Coleman with footprint cast courtesy of Loren Coleman.

Page 114. Bigfoot courtesy of Samuel Faucher.

Page 116. Bigfoot skeleton diagram from a drawing by Bill Munns.

These are the websites I used:

Websites are always changing, so if any of these links stop working, try using a search engine to look up your favorite beasts. But if you're a kid, make sure you ask some grown-up-type person before you search.

The Cryptozoologist: Loren Coleman is one of the world's best-known cryptozoologists. This is his website.
http://www.lorencoleman.com

Cryptomundo: If you want to stay up to date on all the latest cryptozoology news, this is the site for you.
http://www.cryptomundo.com

The Aberdeen Bestiary Project: This site shows the pages from an actual bestiary dated from about 1200 CE.
http://www.abdn.ac.uk/bestiary/

Conrad Gesner's Studies on Animals: This book was written in the 1500s and is considered to be the first modern work of zoology. The whole book is featured online. It has lots of cool pictures.
http://archive.nlm.nih.gov/proj/ttp/flash/gesner/gesner.html

Dave's Mythical Creatures: This site has explanations and illustrations for all kinds of beasts.
http://www.eaudrey.com/myth/

Strange Science: Examples from history of classic goofs by scientists in identifying strange creatures.
http://www.strangescience.net/goof.htm

The Centaur Excavations at Volos: Learn about the creation of the Centaur of Volos.
http://www.lib.utk.edu/aboutlibs/hodges/centaur.html

Bunyips: This is a cool site with just about every known piece of information about the bunyip.
http://www.nla.gov.au/exhibitions/bunyips/

The Munns Report: Bill Munns has compiled all of his research here, to try to prove whether or not the creature in the Patterson-Gimlin Bigfoot film is a man in costume.
http://www.themunnsreport.com/

Pop isn't going to like it that I'm sharing this stuff.

To Mom & Dad, with love.
To my kids, family, friends, colleagues, and most
of all, Ralph, thank you for cheering me on.
I couldn't have done this without you.
—S. B.

To Abigail Thaddeus, wherever you may be.
Thank you for being such a wonderfully inspiring person.
Without your determination, creativity, and humor,
this book would never have been possible.
—R. M.

Published by Charlesbridge
85 Main Street
Watertown, MA 02472
(617) 926-0329
www.charlesbridge.com

Library of Congress Cataloging-in-Publication Data
Brockway, Stephanie.
    Mystic Phyles : beasts / Stephanie Brockway and Ralph Masiello.
        p. cm. — (Diary of Abigail Thaddeus)
    Summary: In her diary, thirteen-year-old Abigail Thaddeus intersperses
revelations from her secret quest to unearth the mysteries of mythological
beasts with reports of the everyday strangeness of her own dysfunctional
life.
    ISBN 978-1-57091-718-9 (reinforced for library use)
[1. Diaries—Fiction. 2. Animals, Mythical—Fiction. 3. Middle schools—
Fiction. 4. Schools—Fiction. 5. Orphans—Fiction. 6. Grandparents—Fiction.]
I. Masiello, Ralph, ill. II. Title. III. Title: Beasts.
PZ7.B7832Mys 2011
[Fic]—dc22   2010035786

Printed in China
(hc) 10 9 8 7 6 5 4 3 2 1

Bestiary Masielus illustrations by Ralph Masiello in oil on paper
All other illustrations by Stephanie Brockway in mixed media
Color separations by Chroma Graphics, Singapore
Printed and bound in February 2011 by Imago in Singapore
Production supervision by Brian G. Walker
Art directed by Susan Mallory Sherman

THE END

Het Einde
(That's Dutch.)

But remember, as always, as I told you at first [that this is all a fairy tale] and only fun and pretense; and therefore, you are not to believe a word of it, even if it is true.

**CHARLES KINGSLEY,
THE WATER BABIES, 1863 CE**

THE
END

Fin
(That's French.)

the end

THE
END

Végén
(That's Hungarian.)

the
end

YES, IT'S REALLY

THE END.

(cue music of doom.) ♪ ♫ ♫ ♫